DATE DUE   JUN 04

GAYLORD			PRINTED IN U.S.A.

Blood Ruby

Blood Ruby

Jan Alexander

This Large Print edition is published by Thorndike Press®, Waterville, Maine USA and by BBC Audiobooks, Ltd, Bath, England.

Published in 2004 in the U.S. by arrangement with Wieser & Elwell, Inc.

Published in 2004 in the U.K. by arrangement with the author.

U.S. Hardcover 0-7862-6344-X (Romance)
U.K. Hardcover 0-7540-9868-0   (Chivers Large Print)

The text of this Large Print edition is unabridged. Other aspects of the book may vary from the original edition.

Set in 16 pt. Plantin by Ramona Watson.

Printed in the United States on permanent paper.

British Library Cataloguing-in-Publication Data available

Library of Congress Cataloging-in-Publication Data

Alexander, Jan, 1937–
    Blood Ruby / Jan Alexander.
       p. cm.
    ISBN 0-7862-6344-X (lg. print : hc : alk. paper)
    1. Inheritance and succession — Fiction.   2. Blessing and cursing — Fiction.   3. Married women — Fiction.
    4. Rubies — Fiction.   5. Large type books.   I. Title.
PS3552.A476B55 2004
813'.6—dc22   2003071119

Blood Ruby

Prologue

Everywhere was smoke, spiraling and swirling, and the sweet, heady scent of incense. In the dim light, dimly perceived through the smoke, one could see half-naked bodies, writhing and twisting to the incessant and muffled beat of a drum. While they danced the worshippers sang, not a song, but an eerie, unsettling chant, sometimes rising on a keening dissonance, then falling again to a shuddering sob. It was ardent music, ardent and unsettling, mysterious like the East from which it came; it was evil. You could almost smell the lust for blood of which they sang.

Clark Rutherford hesitated on the last of the steps leading down. He was not a timid man; he had spent most of his life travelling, and not always to the comfortable, familiar places. He had climbed down into an ancient and cursed tomb of some forgotten pharaoh and looked upon treasures never before seen by Western man. He had hidden in the thick vegetation of a jungle and watched the terrible rites of a man-eating tribe at supper. Once to save his life he had leaped into a river infested with piranhas and swam a hundred feet while arrows tipped with poison parted the waters all about him.

He had looked upon sights that few men could observe with equanimity. He had observed them with curiosity, with interest, with fascination even, but never with anything that he honestly could have called fear.

But here on these rough-hewn steps he paused and actually sniffed the air. This chamber was old; the evil that permeated these stones was ancient evil, stretching back across centuries to mock man's passing virtue.

While he stood there a man appeared before him. There was the odd illusion that the mist had parted for him — a trick, one might say, of the incense and murky light. He wore a hood and a cloak of some deep hue, purple, perhaps, or midnight blue, and this so blended with the dark shadows of the room that he seemed to have no edges, no distinct outline. Only his face could be clearly perceived: swarthy, lined, with intense black eyes and yellowed, rotted-looking teeth.

"Come," he said, and the command was

like another note in the ghastly chant being sung. He motioned and without waiting turned.

Clark followed him. The mists seemed to separate for them, but only just, leaving ghostly tendrils to drift before his eyes or brush like phantom fingers against his cheek.

A low couch had been placed along one wall, and a small table placed near it. A man in western garb was half-reclining on the couch, his eyes closed, a vague smile upon his face. Clark caught a sweet, acrid odor, and thought the man was probably on opium. Perhaps he would not waken; perhaps he would forget why they were here, and this would be a wasted trip after all, albeit a strange one.

But the man opened his eyes as they approached and his smile flickered briefly, more certainly before it faded altogether.

"So you have come," was all he said.

"I told you I would," Rutherford replied. He waited, but nothing more was said. He was aware of that hooded figure hovering at his elbow, and the incessant motion of the dancers. The air had begun to make him lightheaded.

"Have you got it?" he asked finally, suddenly impatient to leave the place.

"The money?" the man on the couch asked.

Rutherford reached to his breast pocket and brought out a packet. He broke the string which tied it and tossed the packet on the couch. It fell open as it landed, and a few green bills slipped out.

To his surprise the man did not count the money, or even reach to pick it up. It was little enough, God knows, if the deal was legitimate; but then, it might not be. For all he knew, someone might put a knife in his back any minute now and take the rest of the money he had brought as insurance in case they raised the price. He repressed an urge to look over his shoulder.

The man on the couch looked at the hooded man and nodded, and he extended one hand toward Rutherford. He opened his fingers, and at once a crimson fire seemed to blaze from the palm of his hand; the fire was a gem, large and beautiful, seeming to burn with a light of its own.

Rutherford gasped; he couldn't believe his eyes. Nothing — none of the legends, nor the talk, nor the stories he had read — had prepared him for this. He hardly dared hold out his hand for it. He could not believe he had gotten this for the pittance he had just tossed onto the couch.

10

"It's magnificent," he whispered, and stretched his hand out. The ruby was dropped into it; for a second the fire that gleamed within it seemed real, seemed to burn his hand. He thought the glow flickered and grew brighter — a trick, no doubt, of the fire in the brazier.

He raised his eyes to meet those of the hooded figure. They were watching him with unnerving intensity.

"Is it mine now?" he asked, still expecting some trick.

The man nodded.

"Can I go?"

Again a nod; he looked toward the couch, and the man there nodded, too. No one spoke. Rutherford thought a ghost of a smile toyed with the corners of the man's mouth.

"Well, then," Rutherford said. This time he could not restrain a nervous glance around. "Thank you," he said. "It has been . . ." he paused, "a rewarding experience," he finished, and allowed himself a smile.

He backed toward the exit, unwilling to turn his back upon them. Neither of them moved. The dancers still danced as oblivious of his presence as if he had been another of the wisps of smoke. The room stank. The wailing was an assault upon the ears.

He reached the steps. The two strangers had all but vanished amid the shadows. He paused for a moment more, then turned quickly and ran up the steps, taking them two at a time. Near the top he stumbled, and it gave him an awful sense of danger, as if it were the moment they had waited for to leap upon him.

But no one pursued him. He reached the street, sucking in great lungsful of air. He still held the ruby in his hand and, suddenly conscious of where he was, he thrust it deep into his pocket and began to walk quickly, senses once again alert for any hint of danger.

For a long moment after Rutherford left the two men stared after him. Then without a word the hooded man left, following slowly after Rutherford. He did not so much as glance at the man on the couch. He had no need to. He knew where to go.

When he was gone the reclining man continued to stare toward the exit for a time. Then with a low groan he sank back upon the couch. He too must go, he knew, but the journey that stretched before him was horrible. He had thought always that when the time came he could face it bravely, but he had deluded himself. No man is without limit to his courage; always there is a terror that surpasses endurance.

He got up from the couch with sudden, jerky movements and staggered toward the door. He collided with one of the dancers.

"Damn you," he muttered and kicked the man out of his way. "Damn you all."

Off in the shadows someone laughed. It made his skin crawl. His legs felt so weak he could hardly walk. By God, he wouldn't run, he would lie down here on the floor and let them come. It would ruin all their fun, wouldn't it?

He half-thought to throw himself on the floor, but the instinct to flee was too great. He made his way to the steps, stumbling up them with one hand and feeling along the mouldy wall.

In the street he went in the direction opposite that taken by Rutherford, hurrying along with a curious broken gait, broken steps, eyes darting ever to and fro.

He had gone no more than a few yards when he heard them behind him, that curious scraping sound, the shuffling, the whisperings. He stopped in his tracks. He didn't look back, he couldn't, he hadn't the guts for that. No man could — knowing what he knew.

He had known it would come, of course, but not when, not so soon.

"They ought to have given me more time," he said, but in his heart he knew they had given all the time they had promised.

He began to run suddenly, loping along, gasping for breath, and always, without listening, without looking, he knew his fate was right behind, that there was no escape; it was as close as his own soul, as close as the terror that hammered in his breast.

As suddenly as he had begun to run, he stopped, standing still on the street, his shoulders heaving with the effort of his breath, tears running from his eyes and spittle from the corner of his mouth.

There was no place to run.

In a nearby room, a sailor was with a girl. Suddenly a scream from the street outside rent the air; on and on it went, rising higher and higher as if in a last desperate reach for Heaven. Then it ended.

"What was that?" the sailor cried, sitting up.

"It was nothing," she murmured, and

reached up for him. She had lived in the quarter for many years. She had heard screams before, more than she cared to remember. She never interfered or went to see. Here, no one ever did.

Chapter 1

"What was that?"

Joseph Hanson set aside his newspaper and cocked his head, listening for a moment. "A carriage," he said, rising. "Are we expecting anyone?"

"Not that I know of," his wife said. She had been embroidering his initials on a handkerchief which she too set aside. It was late, nearly nine o'clock, and company did not often "drop in" on them. "Uncle Clark, perhaps?"

"I wasn't expecting him back until tomorrow." Joseph went to the window and pulled one corner of a curtain aside to peer out. By now the carriage had pulled up in front of the house. He watched a tall, slim man emerge from it, step nimbly to the ground, and all but run up the steps. He turned from the window, letting the curtain flutter back into place.

"Your admirer," he said drily, returning to his chair and his paper.

"Bill?" Liza said, standing.

"Who else?"

She blushed slightly and in her confusion knocked her embroidery to the floor. It was an open secret that Bill Whitney was quite taken with her; anyone with eyes could have seen it in the way he looked at her longingly, the way he clung to every word she spoke. It was amusing to most, annoying to Liza, who thought Bill a nice enough person, if it weren't for his feelings toward her.

She was never quite sure how Joseph felt about the situation; he had never indicated by word or deed that he took it seriously. Both men worked in the offices of Clark Rutherford, who was Joseph's uncle, and this business connection gave Bill various opportunities to call, so that she saw more of him than she would otherwise have permitted.

His interest in her embarrassed her and made her feel strangely guilty. She did not quite know how to cope with it without hurting his feelings unduly. In fact, she loved her husband very much, but she was not by nature a demonstrative person. It would have embarrassed her to go to her husband and reassure him that she loved only him and did not give a fig if Bill Whitney loved her, that indeed, she would much prefer that he did not. So instead she said nothing, and blushed when her husband made his occasional remarks, and hoped that they were made in jest.

The doorbell rang. Ordinarily at this late hour she would have answered it herself, but this time she did not. After a moment she heard Mrs. Morgan's heavy tread on the stairs; the housekeeper had long since gone up to her room, and Liza could well imagine that she would grumble about this unwarranted demand upon her "aching feet," but she came, and in a minute they heard her answer the door. There was a murmur of voices and soon after Bill Whitney came in without waiting to be shown. The autumn air had left his nose red and his face flushed, and he had an eager way about him. His glance ricocheted from Joseph to Liza.

"Clark's back," he said quickly, as if afraid that, with any less important news he would not be allowed to stay.

"Hello, Whitney," Joseph said. "You look cold. Some brandy?"

"Sounds good," Bill said, acknowledging his host's greeting.

"I'll get it," Liza said, glad for an excuse to get away from Bill's look of devotion.

Mrs. Morgan appeared in the doorway

to ask in an aggrieved voice, "Will there be anything else, Missus?"

"Thank you, no," Liza said. "Good night."

"Good night, then," Mrs. Morgan said with finality. Her footsteps pounded heavily up the stairs, each tread a complaint.

"So the old man's back early," Joseph said, taking the glass that his wife brought him.

"He said he'd be along here in a few minutes," Bill said. "Said he had something he wanted to show you."

Joseph cocked an eyebrow. Liza, handing Bill his drink, was careful that their hands did not touch. Bill, she saw, was disappointed.

"Something to show me," Joseph said. "Wonder what it could be."

"Probably some knickknack that he picked up on his journey," Liza said. "You know how he is."

"I ought to," Joseph said. "It's what keeps the company broke and us poor."

It was a familiar complaint. Clark Rutherford was an inveterate traveller and collector. The walls and cabinets of his home were filled with the souvenirs of his travels. There was a parang, a Malay

19

sword, above his sofa, and a suit of armor in the hall. In a case were dueling pistols from France and an opium pipe from China next to an exquisite lacquered bowl from Japan. There were numerous drinking cups and plates, hats and shoes and shawls, daggers and prints and old maps and even, to Liza's continual horror, a shrunken head from somewhere in South America.

"It is his money," she said now in his defense. "I should think he has a right to spend it however he wishes."

"I should think he has an obligation to the company," Joseph said.

"He's promised that one day you'll be in charge," she said. "Then you can do what you want with it."

"If there's anything left," he said.

They were saved a further quarrel by the sound of wheels in the drive, and the opening and closing of a carriage door.

"There he is," she said, starting toward the hall. "Be nice, please, he's probably tired from his trip."

"Mostly I'd say he looked excited," Bill said.

Clark Rutherford was Joseph's uncle, but Liza could not have been more fond of him had he been her own relative. She had lost her father as a child, and she had been quite young when she married Joseph. Clark Rutherford, as much as possible for a man of his gypsy inclinations, had taken her under his wing. The house they lived in was his and he had taken Joseph into his company, with a promise of future promotion to a managing role. Despite her husband's impatience, Liza was rather contented with her lot; she loved her husband and she was quite fond of her uncle, footloose though he might be.

The affection was mutual. Rutherford greeted her with a great hug and a fatherly kiss on the cheek. "Prettier than ever," he decided, holding her at arm's length.

"I'll bet you say that to a girl in every port," she said. "Here, give me your coat."

"Not *every* port," he said. He took off his coat and gloves, rubbing his hands together briefly. She put her arm through his and they went back into the parlor.

Clark Rutherford was a big man, tall and sturdily built. His hair was white but thick and exuberant-looking. It had been red once, and his arms and the backs of his hands still gleamed like copper in the light. Under his thick brows his eyes were keen and intelligent, but rarely unfriendly. There was about him a never-vanishing scent of the sea, of bay rum and tropical flowers and the sweet, heady incense of the east.

The three men exchanged warm greetings. Joseph thought a great deal of "the old man," as he liked to call him, and as usual his impatience melted in the warmth of Rutherford's good cheer.

"You'll not carp when you see what I've got this time," Rutherford said, accepting the brandy Liza brought him; he was well aware that Joseph thought more money should be put into the company, and was quite unaffected by it. "Especially when you hear the price."

"I'm willing to bet it's more than we've got in the account," Joseph said, but good-naturedly.

Rutherford smiled and, reaching into his breast pocket, he removed a small box, the sort of box in which jewelers package rings and small pieces of jewelry. He paused for a moment for effect; then he opened it, and set it on the table before them.

There was a moment of speechlessness, a sucking in of the breath. The three of them — Liza, Joseph, and Bill — stared incredulously at the glowing stone. In the flickering light from the gaslights the ruby seemed to wink mysteriously at them.

"It's lovely," Liza said breathlessly.

"It's magnificent," Joseph said, reaching for the box.

"Eh-eh," Rutherford said, stopping his hand. "Mustn't do that. There's a curse on the thing, you know."

"A curse?" Bill said.

"You don't believe that sort of rot, I hope," Joseph said.

Rutherford shrugged, and retrieved the box from the table. "Maybe, maybe not," he said. "It's the famous Baghdad Ruby. For twenty years, in every corner of the globe, I've heard tales and legends of this stone. I never dared dream it would be mine someday."

"It must have cost a fortune," Joseph said, still awed by the sight of the ruby.

"A thousand dollars. It's worth a hundred times that, at least."

"Are you sure it's genuine?" Bill asked.

There was an odd note of irony in Rutherford's voice as he said, "Oh yes, it's the real thing all right, there's no doubt of that."

"What about the curse?" Liza asked. "And all the legends?"

Rutherford took a sip of his brandy and said, "It's a Burma ruby, of course, you can tell that from the color, a so-called

23

blood ruby. The oldest stories, though, go back to Baghdad in the twelfth century. It belonged to some caliph then, and he was said to be a hundred years old, but he looked no more than thirty."

"I shall have to borrow the stone from time to time over the years," Liza said with a laugh.

"I doubt that you'd want to," Rutherford said. "The stone is said to belong to Eblis, in Muslim legend the king of the wicked jinns, or geniis. That's where it gets its so-called magic powers. It's said to bring a man anything he wants, except happiness."

"But if a man already had that," Joseph said, "The stone would provide everything else he could dream of." He sounded excited by the dreams the legend had conjured up for him.

"It's not quite that simple, unfortunately," Rutherford said. "There's a blood curse on the stone. It's said that everything you obtain through the stone's magic must be paid for in blood — your own, or someone else's. What's more, the stone really belongs, as I said, to Eblis. In return for its use, the owner's soul is traded to the jinn. At the owner's death, which is always tragic, the soul is turned into another jinn — damned for eternity as one of Eblis's evil slaves."

"Well," Liza said, still amused, "I know women who'd consider that a small enough price for eternal youth."

"And some without any souls to begin with," Bill said.

"Anyway," Rutherford said with a rueful smile, putting the stone and its box back into his pocket, "It's too late for me to contemplate keeping my youth. I'll have to settle for wealth, I suppose."

"We could use some of that right now," Joseph said, his thoughts coming back to the present. "As of this morning, we're a little short what we need for the payroll."

"Perhaps I can help."

There was a shattering of glass. Rutherford had dropped his drink at the sound of the strange voice. Liza gasped and turned toward the door to the hall. There was a man there, a stranger. He was tall and gaunt, with a swarthy complexion and rotted teeth which he revealed now in a brief grin. He wore a black suit, but an eastern turban was wound round his head.

How did he get in? was Liza's first thought; the bell had not rung. Had he let himself in?

"Who the devil are you?" Joseph demanded, putting his glass aside loudly.

"I'm sorry, let me do the honors," Rutherford said. He had recovered himself, but he looked shaken and, Liza thought, pale. "My new assistant, Al Zaghral. He's got some excellent ideas for the company. My nephew, Joseph Hanson, and his lovely wife, Liza. And Bill Whitney, office manager for the company."

Al Zaghral bowed to each of them in turn. Liza and Bill responded with polite "How-do-you-do's," but Joseph surveyed the newcomer coldly.

"Your new assistant?" he said. "To take over the company when you retire, no doubt?"

"Now Joseph," Rutherford started to say, but Al Zaghral silenced him with a gesture.

"Please," he said, in his deep, foreign-sounding voice. "You have a right, perhaps, to be suspicious, but let me put your mind at ease. It is my hope, indeed, my intention, that one day I will serve you as I now serve your uncle."

He bowed again. His words, with a ring of sincerity, mollified Joseph, who relaxed somewhat. But Liza had been watching Uncle Clark, and she thought that he started slightly at Al Zaghral's remark.

The easterner approached Rutherford and handed him a small packet. "This came after you left," he said. "I thought that it would be of interest, and so took the liberty of intruding upon this private gathering."

Rutherford tore the package open. Inside, the others could see a large sum of money. Rutherford looked at Al Zaghral questioningly.

"The note with it said it was the payment of a wager," Al Zaghral explained. "It came from a Mr. Patterson."

"Not Gordon Patterson," Joseph said in disbelief.

"The same," Rutherford said. "I saw him on the boat going out. We had some drinks, played some cards. I made a bet . . . but my God, I never expected him to take me seriously. Why, it was all in jest . . ."

He paused; a curious silence had descended upon the others. They were glancing at one another strangely.

"What is it?" Rutherford asked.

"We heard from Gordon's daughter just yesterday," Liza said finally. "Her father . . . he passed away just three days ago."

"He committed suicide," Bill said.

"But why, what on earth for?" Rutherford demanded. "Why, it's not three months since I saw him, and he was in excellent spirits."

"No one knows why," Joseph said. "We'll probably never know. He hung himself, that's all we know."

Rutherford glanced at the package in his hand, and laid it on the table as if reluctant to hold it. "He must have sent this just before it happened," he said.

They all stared distastefully at the packet of money. "Perhaps you should return it to his widow," Liza said. "After all, if you didn't even take the bet seriously —"

"If I may be permitted to interject an opinion," Al Zaghral said. "Mr. Patterson apparently felt the wager was in earnest, or else he would not have sent the money. And, I daresay, it is more than enough to make up the shortage in payroll that was worrying Mr. Hanson just now . . ." He let his voice trail off, and gave Joseph a toothy grin.

There was a lengthy pause. Each of them in turn looked at the money, and then around the room at one another. It was Joseph who finally broke the silence.

"He's right, of course," he said, putting his hand out and gathering up the money. "We do need the cash."

"Still . . ." Rutherford said dubiously.

"You could always regard it as a loan," Al Zaghral said. "Later, if you feel you must, it could be returned to the widow."

"Excellent suggestion," Joseph said. The cash disappeared into his pocket.

Al Zaghral bowed again; there was, although none of them noticed it, the faintest trace of a smile upon his lips.

Chapter 2

Rutherford Mills had been in the family for some time. It was a small company, as such mills went, and it seemed with each year to produce less profit. Clark Rutherford had always been quick to admit that he was no businessman, and he had been content with the modest income the mill provided; if he minded its deteriorating state, he never revealed it. It was Joseph who worked hard and fretted, and not for himself alone.

"Another two or three years like the last two," he had often told Liza, "And Clark Rutherford will find himself out on the streets. The mill didn't make enough last year even to keep the loans paid up."

Liza, who had never had a head for business, listened patiently while Joseph tried to make her see their predicament. But the fact was, she adored his uncle, and regarded her husband as so clever that she retained the conviction all along that things would come out right eventually.

And finally it began to look as if circumstances were proving her right. Business was booming. She had only a vague under-standing of what was going on, but she gathered that Uncle Clark's new assistant, Al Zaghral, had made a number of really useful suggestions. It was almost a year now since he had been there and in that time they had ventured beyond the mere weaving of fabrics; now they were engaged in creating their own line of clothes. She had seen the new dresses and had even been able to make some excellent sugges-tions regarding styles; it was her sole con-tribution to the business.

There was more money and Joseph had ceased to harp on that subject. At his sug-gestion she had had a new wardrobe made for winter; it had been a long time since she had been able to splurge on more than one outfit at a time, and she had had great fun picking fabrics, deciding on designs, going for fittings, and later, modelling all her stylish new clothes for her husband's pleasure.

Why, then, was she unhappy? She asked herself this question one afternoon while she rode in the carriage through streets made clean by new-fallen snow. It was only a few weeks from Christmas. Joseph had given her an extremely generous allowance for Christmas shopping and, when she remarked on his ever-increasing absences, he had given her a puppy, a floppy-eared spaniel who sat beside her on the seat just now.

"To cure your loneliness," he had said, and kissed her warmly. She had kissed him back warmly, had adored the puppy — and had continued to be unhappy.

"There," she told herself, pressing her nose against the cold glass and watching the steam obscure the view, "You've already said it. It's because he's gone so much."

But even this simple explanation did not quite satisfy. There was something else, something she could not quite put her finger on.

The dog nuzzled her elbow, hungry for some attention, and she sighed and opened her arm so that he could crawl into her lap.

"Erasmus," she said, "Why do you think I'm melancholy?"

His answer was to curl into a contented ball, his nose buried in the fur of her muff. She patted his head absent-mindedly.

It was this feeling of vague discontent that had brought her out that day to the mill. She never went there as a rule. She told Joseph it was because she objected to all the noise and the dust, but in fact what she objected to was the empty-eyed look of the workers, many of them little children. She had seen boys of eight and nine working in torn clothes and bare feet, and she had seen the hollow, dulled looks they gave her as she passed.

"But aren't there laws against children working?" she had asked Joseph after her first visit.

He shrugged. "There are," he said, "But no one pays them any attention. Children work in all the mills. And look at it this way, these children have to help support their families. Believe me, we wouldn't be doing them any favors by dismissing them."

She had had to admit that he was right in that; still, the sight of them, so solemn, so unchildlike, haunted her for several days after each visit, and she had finally made up her mind to avoid the place.

The carriage stopped. She looked distastefully out the window at her destination. It had been snowing off and on for two days before, but the traffic around the mill had turned the snow into a muddy slush. Between the carriage and the door to the office building lay a sea of mud and slush. Someone had made a walkway of boards, but its narrow width was not intended to protect a lady's flowing skirts. She crinkled her nose in disgust and stepped down, holding her skirts as high as modesty permitted.

In those bleak surroundings she stood out like a precious gem. Her gown and the pert little hat atop her head were of amethyst velvet, and she carried a mink muff, an extravagance Joseph had insisted upon for her. There was another little puff of fur to match it at the collar of her jacket.

She was an exceptionally pretty girl, with her hair falling in masses of dark ringlets about her shoulders. She had an alabaster complexion, and wide, grey eyes that sparkled gaily when she was amused. Her laugher was like the ripple of a valley brook when the sun has shone on the mountain snow all day long. Her waist was tiny, her hands exquisite. Wherever she went, admiring glances went with her.

There were other glances that followed her as she gingerly traversed the board path, glances that were sullen and resentful, even hateful. There were women about whose hands, calloused and old before their time, had never touched velvet, and the looks they gave her new dress were anything but admiring. There were men who wouldn't be warm until the summer sun shone on them again, and they saw the little mink muff and the mink collar, and their lust was not for her tiny waist nor her little painted mouth.

Her husband and Bill Whitney were in the midst of a heated discussion regarding some financial question. Bill looked pleased to see her; Joseph did not. He gave her a perfunctory kiss and asked what brought her out on a cold morning.

"A desire to see my husband," she said. "In the last week-and-a-half I've seen you twice at dinner, and some nights not at all. I've begun to think I'll have to take a job at the mill if I want to spend any time with you."

"What would you have me do?" he asked with a sigh. "Your favorite uncle keeps buying and expanding, expanding and buying. I almost think I liked it better when he spent his time travelling."

"It seems so unlike Uncle Clark," Liza said. "What do you suppose has gotten into him? I haven't seen him in two months at least, and he used to stop by at least once a week."

"It's that blasted ruby," Joseph said, resentment creeping into his voice.

"Now, Joe, you know that's a lot of malarky," Bill said.

"Is it?" Joseph asked. "When he brought it back with him he said he wanted wealth. And since then everything he's touched has turned to gold."

"He also said everything acquired through the stone's magic had to be paid in blood," Liza said lightly, hoping to tease her husband into a better mood; she attached little importance to the ruby Uncle Clark had acquired. Envy was not one of her faults and she certainly did not believe in magic.

"Well, he's paying for his new wealth in my blood," Joseph said. "Look, darling, if there's anything you want, Bill will take care of it for you. I've got to look at some new equipment they're setting up."

She glanced vaguely around the office. "Is there anything I can do to help?" she asked.

"Yes," he said. "Get me the Baghdad ruby." He said it with a laugh, but there was an undertone that suggested he was not altogether joking.

He gave her another perfunctory kiss. She did not point out that Bill could not assuage her loneliness. "Will I see you at dinner?" she asked instead.

"Maybe," was his reply. He went out, leaving her as dissatisfied as when she had arrived. She stared unhappily at the door through which he had disappeared.

"It's not his fault," Bill said sympathetically. "The old man's really kept him hopping."

"He's spoken so often of that ruby," she said, more to herself than to Bill. "I sometimes think he's become obsessed with it."

"It's just that it symbolizes the old man's new-found wealth," Bill said.

She turned thoughtfully to Bill. "Is Uncle Clark really so wealthy?" She had never thought of their increased spending money in that light before.

Bill laughed drily. "Very," he said.

"And he wasn't before?"

"No, this is all sudden. That's why your husband has been so busy, and a bit irritable."

"What were you two arguing about when I came in?" she asked. She did not care to listen to another's complaints about her husband's irritability, even if she secretly agreed with them.

"This," he said, tapping a stack of legal-looking documents, "the old man's latest acquisition — a bank."

"A bank? What on earth does he want with a bank?"

Bill shrugged. "Who knows? It's funny.

This bank used to virtually own the mill through all their loans. Now we own them. Sort of the tail wagging the dog, isn't it?"

She did not pretend to understand financial matters, but she could not help being awed by the sudden change in Clark Rutherford's financial status. Before it had meant nothing more than the absence of her husband, and money to spend on a new wardrobe. Now she began to see the bigger picture. She told herself that it ought to make her happy, but somehow she found it strangely disquieting.

"I guess I'd better go," she said. Bill saw her to the door; for once she did not object to his attention.

Her first discovery when she came out was that the carriage door had blown open, and Erasmus had gotten out. She found him at a glance. It was lunchtime at the mill, and one of the workers, a boy of about ten, was seated on the low rail fence nearby. An open book and a half-eaten piece of bread were in his lap, but for the moment his attention was all on the spaniel puppy. The two, boy and dog, seemed quite delighted with their new friendship.

When he saw her coming, though, the boy's smile vanished, to be replaced by a vacant stare. He folded his hands primly in his lap, ignoring Erasmus's efforts to renew their play.

"I didn't let him out, ma'am," he said before she could say a word to him. "First thing I know'd he was here in front of me begging for a bit of lunch."

"It was kind of you to share your lunch with him," she said. "But you musn't let him talk you out of all of it. He eats quite well at home, I assure you."

"I expect dogs and boys are hungry all the time," he said solemnly. The remark gave her a pang; she wondered if this poor young creature ever had enough to eat to assuage his hunger. Yet there was a proud set to his chin and in his voice.

"Isn't it quite cold to eat out here?" she asked.

"I'm eatin' out here 'cause Ma's feeling poorly," he said. There was no trace of expression in his face.

She glanced toward the mill. "Does your father work at the mill?" she asked. Having struck up the conversation, she was reluctant now to simply walk away. There was something pathetic about the little urchin that touched her. She longed to see him smile or to hear him laugh as a boy his age should. She found his solemn gaze unnerving.

"Pa's dead," he said. "There's just Ma and Jessie and me."

"Jessie's your sister?"

"Yes, ma'am," he said.

"And I suppose that's for her," she said. Near him atop the fence was a half-carved stick doll and a pocket knife.

"Yes, ma'am she's always said she wanted a doll, and I thought I'd make her one for Christmas."

She thought of the dolls she had enjoyed as a little girl, most of them still packed away in a trunk in the attic. She felt a pang of guilt that she should have been so much more fortunate, and wondered if there were some way she could share what she had with this family without wounding what was obviously a strong sense of pride.

"And what is your name?" she asked.

"Glade," he said. "Glade Conners."

Erasmus, bored with the conversation and despairing of the rest of Glade's bread, jumped up at Liza, leaving muddy prints on the front of her skirt. She reached down and picked him up, heedless of the damage he was doing.

"Well," she said, since the conversation seemed at a dead end. "I'll have to go now. It was nice talking to you."

"Good-bye," he said, his eyes watching

the eager kisses Erasmus was bestowing upon her cheek.

When she was in the carriage and driving away, Liza found herself looking back. Young Glade Conners, having seemingly forgotten her, was already at work again on the stick doll for his sister Jessie.

The picture he made, sitting on the fence, carving so solemnly, stayed with her.

Chapter 3

The next day Liza again traveled to the mill. The previous afternoon, on arriving home, she had gone almost at once to the attic and, rummaging through old trunks and boxes, had come up with the doll that had been her favorite as a child. She had brought it down to the parlor, where she left it sitting atop a carved table. Beside it she put a stack of books she used to read — *Black Beauty, Little Men,* and *The Scottish Chiefs.*

Joseph had not come home until after she was in bed, but this weighed less heavily on her than it sometimes did, and the next morning she was surprised to catch herself humming as she dressed.

"My, I do seem to have recaptured my good spirits," she said to herself. She was not a particularly introspective person and it did not occur to her that this was because she had taken an interest in something outside herself and her own immediate world.

It was during the work shift when she arrived at the mill and she did not see Glade sitting on the rail fence, nor did he enter the mill as the day before. This time she went toward the rows of houses in which the mill workers lived.

These sat on a slope; the streets between the houses, if streets they could be called, were streams of slimy mud in which several grubby-looking little children were playing. By asking directions of these Liza was able to find the house in which the Conners family lived.

This was a house like all the others, a plain box, unpainted, with a meager stoop the only relief to its flat exterior. Her arms filled with packages, Liza tapped at the door with her foot and almost at once it was opened by a wide-eyed little girl.

"Hello," Liza said, smiling brightly down on the waif, "you must be Glade's little sister, Jessie."

The girl nodded mutely, awed by the presence of this beautiful and elegant woman at their humble door.

"Is your mother at home?" Liza asked, and when the child nodded again, "May I come in?"

At almost the same moment a woman's voice from inside the house said, "Jessie, show the lady in."

The interior of the house was dim. A

blanket had been hung over one window, to cut the drafts, perhaps, or to keep out the light. For a moment Liza could see nothing. Finally she made out a thin woman sitting in a rocking chair across the room. The woman tried to rise, but she was seized with a coughing spell and sank helplessly back into the chair.

"Oh, don't try to get up, please," Liza cried, crossing the room. "Glade said you had been feeling poorly."

The woman looked up at her with Glade's solemn eyes, but there was a look of distrust in them, too. "You must be the pretty lady he said he talked to," she said. "The one with the dog."

"Yes," Liza said. "But I didn't bring Erasmus today. May I sit down?"

Mrs. Conners nodded toward a wooden chair nearby and Liza seated herself. She put the books on the floor, where she thought Glade would eventually find them himself. The doll was in a box and this she held out toward Jessie, who had continued to stare at her in awe.

"I found this among some old things," she said, "and as Glade mentioned having a sister, I thought perhaps you could get some use out of it."

Jessie took the box hesitantly and lifted

44

the lid. She gave a little cry, and seized the doll from within the box.

"Oh, it's beautiful," she cried hugging the doll to her breast.

"I'm sorry, but we don't take charity," Mrs. Conners said.

Liza, who had been thrilled at the sight of the child's delight, was crestfallen. She hadn't counted on the Conners's pride.

"Mrs. Conners," she said, "It isn't meant to be charity. I have no use for the doll myself, and it seems a shame to just throw it away when it's still useful. Surely you can see that."

The stubborn set of Mrs. Conners' chin softened a little. "Well," she said uncertainly.

"Can't I keep it, Ma, please?" Jessie pleaded.

"I suppose it's all right, just this once," Mrs. Conners said relenting.

Liza breathed a silent sigh of relief and for the first time glanced around the interior of the house. It was filled with boxes and cartons and stacks of personal belongings.

"Why, you're getting ready to move," she said aloud, surprised.

"Yes, ma'am," Mrs. Conners said. Jessie had retired to the corner by the window, where she was lovingly examining her new playmate.

"I hope you'll wait until you're feeling better," Liza said. "It wouldn't do to overtax yourself when you're poorly."

"We wasn't asked to move, ma'am," was the reply, "We was told we had to, by tomorrow."

"But that's ridiculous," Liza said. "It's turned quite cold, and it's obvious to anyone that you're in no condition right now to make such a move."

Mrs. Conners made no reply to this, but only sat and stared solemnly at her; perhaps she felt she had already said too much. Liza had never introduced herself, but like the other workers Mrs. Conners knew her at sight. It was partly for this reason she had given in on the question of the doll. No one who worked at the mills could afford to offend a relative of the owner, even one whose position in the family hierarchy was as vague as Liza's.

"Mrs. Conners," Liza said, standing, "I know very little about these things, but I am certain that the housing of the millworkers is under my husband's management. I give you my assurance I shall speak to him about this. Never mind about moving tomorrow — the order shall be rescinded, at least until your health is better."

Mrs. Conners still made no reply beyond, "We appreciate your interest, ma'am," but neither her words nor her manner indicated that she had any faith in the success of Liza's efforts.

Liza left them, making no mention of the books she had brought for Glade. She did not feel up to coaxing Mrs. Conners to accept them, too; no doubt Glade would find them, and perhaps he could make it right with his mother.

She found Bill Whitney in the office, but Joseph was nowhere to be seen.

"He's in the mill, or maybe the warehouse," Bill said. "What's bothering you? You looked all riled up about something."

She told him briefly about the visit to the Conners's house and the reason for wanting to see her husband. "It just isn't right, Bill," she said firmly, "That woman isn't well enough to move, anyone can see that at a glance."

Bill had looked a bit embarrassed as she talked, and now he said, "There are a lot of things that aren't quite right in the way the workers are treated. But at least here they had been treated better than other mills."

"Had been?" Liza said.

His embarrassment deepened. He shrugged and said, "There have been a lot of changes around here lately."

"I want to talk to Joseph," Liza said stubbornly.

"It won't do any good, Liza," Bill said with a sigh. "Joseph isn't kicking that family out. Joseph's always bent over backward to be lenient to the workers. There are families that were supposed to be evicted a year ago that are still where they were, two or three families that aren't even supplying any workers any more. Rutherford Mills has always been soft about enforcing the rules. Like, the number of workers a family supplies is supposed to determine how many rooms they have. That's why the Conners family has to move. The father died six months ago, and now they aren't entitled to such a big house anymore."

"But if they've been allowed to stay six months," Liza said, "Why is it imperative that they move tomorrow?"

"It's the old man," Bill said. "He ordered Joseph to get the housing straightened out and up-to-date. With all the expansion, there are lots of new workers being hired, and they need all the housing they can find."

"Then why not put up new housing?"

Bill hesitated for a moment. "I guess they plan to do that, too," he said lamely.

"But that takes time, I suppose."

"It's easier, no doubt, to force families from their homes," Liza said angrily.

"Anyway, it's no use complaining to Joseph, he fought the old man on this, but his uncle was set on it. If you're going to fight with anyone about it, you'll have to go see him."

"Maybe I will at that," Liza said. "Is he in his office?"

Bill looked surprised by the question. "Why, no, he hardly ever comes in anymore," he said. "He runs things from home."

"I didn't know," Liza said thoughtfully, reflecting for a moment on the extent of things she did not know. But she said with determination, "Very well, then, I shall go to see him at home."

Clark Rutherford lived at Sea Cliff, a monstrous structure that sprawled across the cliffs overlooking the ocean's rocky shore. Liza had always thought it hideous, but its uniqueness somehow made it seem right for Uncle Clark.

Lately she had seen even less of Clark Rutherford than of her husband. He had been accustomed in the past to dropping in frequently, but since his return from his last trip, the one in which he had acquired that lovely ruby, she had hardly seen him at all. He had been totally absorbed in his miraculously booming business, she supposed. It had been at least six weeks since she had last talked with him, and then he had been abrupt and preoccupied.

Now, as the carriage wound its way up the long drive that led to Sea Cliff, she experienced a pang of guilt in not coming before. Suppose he had been sick — he was no longer a young man, after all — and she, his thoughtless relative, had not bothered with him at all, until she had complaints to make.

If the problem of the Conners had not been so immediate she would have let it go for another visit and kept this one purely social.

"But he has always been receptive to anyone's problems," she reassured herself, alighting from her carriage.

Wallace, Uncle Clark's man, had been with him as long as Liza could remember. He was pleased to see her and asked politely after her health, but when she asked if Uncle Clark was in, the butler looked embarrassed and even at a loss.

"He's not having visitors," he said, with the goodness to stammer a little.

"But why?" Liza asked, bewildered. Since she had met Clark Rutherford she had always been welcomed here with open arms. She could not think why, busy or not, that should have changed. "Wallace, is he ill?" she asked.

"Miss, I . . ." The butler said and paused. "He's simply not having visitors," he finished lamely.

"He will have one," Liza said stubbornly. "I have come to see him, and see him I shall, if only to see for myself whether he is well or ill. Is he in his room?"

She started around the hesitant butler, and would have gone directly up the stairs, but Uncle Clark's voice, coming from the little library off the hall, stopped her.

"It won't be necessary to go up, my dear," he called, "I'm in here. Do come in, please."

"Sir," Wallace said, stepping to the doorway.

"It's all right, Wallace, I shall take full blame," Liza said, sweeping past him into the room. But within she came to a full stop.

Clark Rutherford was seated in a massive chair whose wings swept out to shelter him. Its size dwarfed him, but the impression was that he had shrunk.

He looked ghastly. Despite his years he had always looked healthful and young, and his skin had been hardly lined at all. But now his flesh hung in sallow folds and his eyes were dark hollows. His hair, so luxuriant before, lay in limp strands across his forehead and his hands, folded upon the head of a walking stick, trembled so badly that she could see it from across the room.

She could not have hidden her surprise and dismay had she tried, and for a full moment she stood where she was, staring at him. At last he gave a sardonic chuckle.

"Well," he said, "did you only come to admire my appearance?"

"Uncle Clark," she said, hurrying across to him, "You've been ill, and I didn't know, no one told me. Can you ever forgive me for not coming sooner?"

"I'm all right," he said sharply, and when she would have put a hand to his forehead he shoved it rudely away. "I'm all right," he said again. "Sit down, Liza, don't fuss."

His tone was so sharp, his manner so rude, that she was struck dumb. She backed away from him and bumped into a chair. Absent-mindedly she did as he bade, and sat in it.

She could hardly believe her eyes. He

had aged ten, even twenty years. He looked as if the life-blood, the very soul, had been sucked from him, leaving him dry and only half-alive.

"What has happened to you?" she asked, concerned despite his rudeness.

"What do you care?" he snapped. "Never mind, it is my affair. What brings you here that is so important you must shove past my man and demand to see me? Haven't they told you I'm busy? My affairs have grown in the last few months."

"Yes, I've heard that," Liza said, trying to retain her own humor in the face of his extremely bad one. "But my rudeness was not prompted by selfish motives. I was concerned —"

"For whom?" he interrupted her.

"Why, for you, in the first place, and then for a family who works for you in the second," she said.

"I expect they were in the first place, and I in the second," he said. He gave another sardonic laugh that ended in a violent coughing spell. She would have risen and come to him again, but he waved her away.

"Well, who is this family?" he asked when he had regained his voice. "And exactly what is their problem?"

In the face of his bad mood she would

have preferred not even to discuss the matter with him, but having broached the subject already she could see no diplomatic way to avoid continuing. She told him briefly and as concisely as possible why she had come.

"I would like you to let the Conners stay on, for a week or so at least," she finished lamely.

He regarded her with such a hostile expression that her heart sank even lower. "The Conners family," he said at last. "I know them. They're lucky I don't throw them out on the street altogether."

"Uncle Clark —" she began helplessly, but he would not let her speak.

"The housing for the workers is determined by their value to the mill," he said. "By the number of workers the family provides. But this family . . . The father died months ago. The mother is unable to work. The daughter is too young to work. There's no one but the boy. Do you think the work of one ten-year-old boy is a fair exchange for a four-room house?"

"It need only be for a few weeks," she said. "A few days even. Surely —"

"I need the house," he said.

She felt her face turning red at his continued rudeness. She got to her feet, annoyed to discover that her voice was unsteady.

"Is there no way I can persuade you to give this unfortunate family a few days grace?" she asked.

"None," he said shortly.

"If I may be permitted to make a suggestion?"

It was Al Zaghral's voice. Liza whirled about, startled by the unexpected sound. He was standing in a shadowy corner. Had he been there all along? She had not noticed him when she came in, and yet surely he had not entered the room since she had.

"If I may," he said again, coming forward. He smiled at Liza, a strangely discomforting smile, and addressed himself to Clark Rutherford.

"This house that the family is in," he said, speaking softly and smoothly, "It is a four-room house, yes?"

Rutherford only nodded quickly. He looked angry, but Liza saw that he didn't interrupt his assistant as he had interrupted her.

"And these rooms have doors, do they not?" the Oriental went on. Again a nod. "Then," he said, "Why cannot this family move into two of the rooms where they are, and close off the others, which can

55

then be made available to a second family? There are two entrances, are there not?"

"Why, yes," Liza said, picturing the houses in her mind. "They all have two entrances, a front one, and one through the kitchen, in the back or on the side. Uncle Clark, this is a solution, isn't it? The Conners family wouldn't have to move, and you'd be wasting no housing."

For a long moment Clark Rutherford did not answer. He stared up at his assistant, who continued to smile ingratiatingly; then he looked at Liza. It gave her a start. It seemed to her that Clark Rutherford stared at her with a look of pure hatred.

In a moment it was gone, so that she was afterward able to wonder if she had imagined it altogether. His face was suddenly void of all expression.

"I suppose it is," he said.

"Then may I tell the Conners family they need only collect their things in two of the rooms?" she asked.

"I shall see that it is attended to," Al Zaghral said to her.

"Thank you," she said. She felt guilty that she could not make her thanks sound more sincere; she knew she ought to be grateful to the man, it was his intercession that had gotten what she wanted. But there was something about him that bothered her, that actually filled her with disgust and with . . . yes, she had not wanted to admit it before, but with *fear*. She dreaded any moment with him, and lived in terror of the prospect that at some time, for some reason, he might actually *touch* her. So far that had never happened, but there was something in the way he looked at her . . .

Rutherford suddenly leaned back against the wing of his chair and said, "And now will you leave me, please? I feel tired."

She wanted to ask what she could do to help him; in the past she would gladly have stayed and nursed him back to health, but he had made it plain that he did not want her company, that she could only say lamely "I hope you are feeling better soon," and make her departure.

In the carriage on her way home, a wave of depression settled upon her. She could hardly believe the scene she had just experienced, or the change that had occurred in Uncle Clark.

She had always adored him. Oh, she was willing to concede to her husband that he was no businessman, and no doubt he would have soon spent himself broke. But he had been gentle and kind and fun to be with. He had held life warmly in the palm of his hand and gotten his full measure of happiness from it while hurting no one but, perhaps, himself.

And now, he held life in a stranglehold, choking it to extract each last drop of profit from it. Had it not been so obviously him — his voice, his face, despite its ravaged condition — she would not have believed this could be the same man.

How could he have changed so much? What had happened to him, and when?

She thought back to the last time she had seen him. He had looked tired then, and gaunt. And before that, when he had returned from the East . . .

The East. The trip in which he had hired Al Zaghral, and purchased the Baghdad ruby. She thought of the gem, so magnificent, so legendary.

Clark Rutherford had gained the wealth he had laughingly said he desired. But in exchange he had traded his humanity, his kindness, his gentleness, everything that had made him good and admirable.

She put her face in her hands and wept.

Chapter 4

"Well, it looks as if we've recovered our spirits," Mrs. Morgan said. She was balancing a breakfast tray and trying to kick the door shut with one foot.

"A little," Liza said, smiling. It was three days since she had seen Uncle Clark, and she had spent that time in a despondent state, but this morning she had wakened with a new resolution. Whatever had happened to Uncle Clark, he was still dear to her, and she *would* get to the bottom of it. She would go to him today, with Joseph, and she would not leave again until she had learned the truth.

This decision, once made, gave her new purpose, and when she had eaten her breakfast — for the first time in three days without Mrs. Morgan's scolding — she began to plan her campaign. It was no use trying to invite Uncle Clark for dinner; if he were in the same frame of mind as before, he would only decline. She would do what she had done the last time, just show up at his door and count on her determination, and Joseph's presence, to get them inside.

She had berated her husband for his failure to bring his uncle's condition to her attention. "Heaven only knows how long he's been ill, or how seriously," she complained. "And no one said a word to me, as if it were a deep secret."

"Frankly I've had so much on my mind I only half-noticed myself," Joseph said. "You know how it is, you see someone every day, and you're the last person to notice any change in them."

"How could you not notice?" she asked.

He shrugged. "I certainly noticed the change in his mental outlook. It's puzzled me, too. But things have been booming for him, and some men are like that — a little money, a little success, it goes to their heads, they become hungry for more and more."

"And you think that's what happened to Uncle Clark?" she asked.

"Who's to say? God knows in the last two months he has certainly been greedy enough — and the more he wants, the more he gets."

"I can't understand it," she said.

"If only I had the stone," Joseph said, more to himself than to her. She could not see how this applied to their present conversation and concluded, not for the first time, that her husband's attention was at least half somewhere else.

"And yet," she said, following her own train of thought, "The Conners were allowed to move into two rooms, as his assistant suggested. So Uncle Clark after all is not entirely changed."

In the end Joseph, who was, for all his preoccupation, not an unkind man or an uncaring one, agreed to her suggestion that he come home at midday the following day and accompany her to Uncle Clark's where they were to take a firm stand against his remaining any longer without proper attention.

So Liza was uncommonly vexed when, on the following day, just at midday, Mrs. Morgan announced that two men had come to see Joseph. When they were shown into the parlor she saw that they were strangers; business associates, she supposed. They asked if her husband was home.

"No, not yet," she said, hesitating before adding, "I'm expecting him soon, though, if you'd care to wait."

To her further annoyance one of them said, "If it's no trouble. We tried to catch him at the mill but we just missed him. They said he was coming straight home."

Just as well I told the truth, then, she thought, and invited them to have a seat in the parlor. She saw one of them reach toward his breast pocket, and hesitate.

"Please," she said, rightly guessing that the pocket held a pipe. "Smoke if you'd like."

The man looked relieved, and withdrew the pipe, but a further search of that and his other pockets failed to produce any matches.

"I'll get some," Liza said, persisting in her cheerful manner although it was becoming increasingly plain to her that the gentlemen, whatever the nature of their business with Joseph, were planning a lengthy stay, which would surely undo all her plans for visiting Uncle Clark.

She went to her husband's room for matches, knowing for certain there would be some there. She found them atop his dresser, and was about to turn about to return to the parlor and the visiting strangers when something else atop the dresser caught her eye.

It was a small box, such as jewelers put rings in; it struck her as familiar, although she could not remember Joseph's buying any jewelry since they were married. Curious, and thinking he had perhaps splurged upon a ring for himself, she picked up the box and opened it.

She gasped and nearly dropped the box; within, gleaming red and brilliant, was the ruby, the Baghdad ruby that belonged to Uncle Clark. It was like a warning light, strangely ominous.

She heard footsteps on the stairs. In a panic of guilt she snapped the box shut and placed it atop the dresser again. She did not know why she was so frightened of being seen with the gem in her hand, nor even why the sight of the ruby had frightened her so. It was Uncle Clark's, of course, but there was no reason why Joseph should not have it temporarily in his possession. He worked as an assistant to his uncle, after all; perhaps Uncle Clark had given it to him to take to the jewelers, to discuss possible mountings. Perhaps . . . But would Uncle Clark have parted with that ruby, even for a day? And why hadn't Joseph mentioned to her that he had it? He had talked so often about it that she had begun to wonder if he were obsessed with the thought of the ruby.

And now there it was, on his dresser, and not a word of explanation.

By the time Joseph appeared in the doorway, she was already nearly there herself, far from the dresser and the puzzling box with the gem inside. Nor did she venture to voice aloud the questions that had flashed through her mind.

"There are some men to see you," she said, a trifle breathlessly. "I was looking for some matches . . ."

His glance went briefly beyond her. "Yes, I know, they said you'd come up," he said.

"I'm afraid they'll make us late," she said, avoiding his eyes. "Uncle Clark —"

"It's already too late for Uncle Clark, it would seem," he said.

There was an odd note in his voice that made her, after all, look directly at him. "Why, what do you mean?" she asked. She saw for the first time that her husband too looked drawn and tired. It had been easy to note in Uncle Clark because she had not seen him for such a long time, and he had changed so drastically. But Joseph too was showing the signs of fatigue and strain. Uncle Clark's new prosperity had cost him, too.

"Uncle Clark is dead," Joseph said.

For a moment she was speechless, uncomprehending. She stared dumbly at her husband, her head tilted back because he was so close.

"Dead?" she echoed after a moment. He nodded.

All the stiffness seemed to go out of her at once. She seemed to sag, and she was grateful when Joseph put his arm about her and drew her against his chest.

"Dead," she said again. "Oh, Joseph, if only I had known sooner, if only I had done something when I was there. He should have had a doctor, he should have gone to the hospital. I could see at a glance he was ill, and I did nothing."

"There's no point in blaming yourself," he said, patting her shoulder.

After a moment she remembered their company downstairs. "Those men," she said, glancing up at him again.

"They're from the police department," he said, regarding her steadily.

"The police? But why?" She paused. Something in his expression stopped her.

"Uncle Clark was murdered," he said. "That's why I said there was no point in blaming yourself."

It was a long moment before she could collect her wits. At first she thought, he is joking; but it was too macabre a subject for joking, and another glance at his face told her he was not. Uncle Clark was dead, and not only dead, but murdered.

"But who . . . why?" she stammered. Suddenly she saw the obvious answer. "That awful man," she said. "That new assistant of his . . ."

Joseph again drew her into his embrace. "Darling, we can't start accusing people without knowing the facts," he said, with maddening good sense.

"But he's so awful, you know what I mean, he's always, always —" She broke off into a crying bout, her shoulders shaking as she gave vent to her grief. Joseph held her and patted her shoulder affectionately.

Downstairs the two policemen waited with ill-concealed impatience.

When Liza and Joseph descended the stairs some fifteen minutes later, she was again the self-composed mistress of the house. Only the red rims around her eyes revealed that she had been grief-stricken by the news of Clark Rutherford's death.

Joseph had told her no more than was necessary: Clark had been murdered rather brutally. His body had been found at Sea Cliff, on the floor in the parlor; he had been beaten with a sharp instrument. In fact, his flesh had been all but torn from his body, as if by the claws of some great beast, but out of respect for his wife's sensitivities Joseph had not deemed it necessary to go into the gory details.

Mrs. Morgan was just admitting Bill Whitney as they came down. Liza saw with gratitude that his eyes were red, too; he had worked for Uncle Clark since he was a boy, and he had been more fond of the old man than he would ever have been willing to show.

"Liza — you've heard, then?" he said. He came straight to her and despite the fact that Joseph was beside her, he took her hands into his. "I was afraid . . . some policemen wanted to see Joseph — I sent them here, then I got to thinking, what if you hadn't heard, you wouldn't want to get it from them — so . . ." His voice trailed off as he saw the two policemen standing inside the parlor.

"Well, it looks as if we've got everybody together, or almost everybody," one of the policemen said. "I'm Inspector Berthold, this is Inspector Marks. I wonder if we couldn't have just a minute of your time now?"

Liza saw that he still held his unlit pipe in one hand. For a perverse reason she would not have understood herself, she did not offer him the matches she had gone for originally; she dropped them instead into Joseph's pocket.

Inspector Berthold carried on most of the conversation. He was a thick-bodied man with a large mustache that almost joined with his bushy sideburns. As if to compensate, the top of his head was hairless. Inspector Marks was a thin, nondescript man with thick glasses; he looked more like a mathematics professor than a policeman.

Inspector Berthold addressed Liza. "You know of Mr. Rutherford's death? Well, then — I am sorry, of course. You understand, it is necessary that we ask a few questions. Perhaps it will help us to find the guilty party."

To Joseph he said, "I wonder if you could tell me, sir, how you spent last evening?"

Joseph replied, "I worked until about seven, I came directly home, and spent the rest of the evening with my wife — of late I haven't had much time to spend with her. We retired at ten o'clock."

"And when did you last see your uncle?"

"Yesterday afternoon, about three o'clock. He asked me to come to his house. There were matters he wished to discuss.

He did not often come into the office of late. When he wanted to go over business matters, I usually saw him at his home."

The Inspector turned to Bill. "And you, sir," he said, "Perhaps you would be so kind as to tell us about your evening?"

"There's not much more to tell," Bill said. "I left the mill at six, I ate dinner — it's my usual restaurant, anyone there can identify me. I left there, oh, I suppose seven-thirty, I went directly home. I spoke to my landlady when I came in, so she can tell you what time that was, probably."

"And you did not go out again?" the Inspector asked.

"Not until this morning."

There was a silence. The Inspector had made some notes in a little notebook, and he now seemed to be studying these. Without looking up, he said, "Can anyone suggest a motive for murdering Clark Rutherford?"

"What are the usual motives?" Joseph asked, a trifle impatiently. "Someone after money? A quarrel over a business matter, perhaps? An old grudge?"

The Inspector fixed his keen eyes on him. "Mr. Hanson," he said levelly, "Your uncle's murder does not suggest an ordinary motive. He was almost brutally killed, torn apart, one could almost say —"

"Sir, my wife is a sensitive woman," Joseph said.

The Inspector turned his shrewd eyes on her. Of all the people in the room, he rather liked the wife; what's more, if he was to put his money on anyone to come through a difficult time, it would be her, although he didn't think she had yet discovered how strong she was. She had been crying. Despite her composure, he thought the news had taken her rather aback — or *something* had.

"My apologies," he murmured aloud.

"So far as I know," Bill Whitney said, fixing a resentful gaze on Joseph, "there's only one person who had a real motive for killing the old man."

Unperturbed, Joseph said, "I suppose you mean me."

"You are his heir," Bill said. "Everything goes to you. And you've always resented the way the old man ran things, and the fact that you were just another employee —"

"Bill!" Liza said sharply. "You've no right to talk like that. It's ridiculous, Joseph could never have done such a thing."

"Why not?" Inspector Berthold asked casually.

"Because, for one thing, he was fond of his uncle," she snapped, turning on him,

"And for another, he was with me last evening, as he's already told you."

"I haven't yet said that Mr. Rutherford was murdered last evening," the Inspector said.

"But that is the time you have questioned us about," she said.

He nodded his head and barely restrained a smile. "You retired at ten, is that correct?" he asked.

"The clock was striking as we went up," she said.

"Mrs. Hanson, let me ask you — is it possible that after retiring your husband might have gotten up and gone back out say, between ten and eleven? Without your knowing it?"

She blushed despite her efforts not to. "No, he could not have gone out between ten and eleven without my knowing it," she said.

The Inspector did not pursue that line. "There is one thing more," he said, referring again to his notes. "Something is missing — at least, we have not yet found it. Perhaps you can help us. It is my understanding that Mr. Rutherford recently made a purchase, a gem, a rather special ruby . . ."

It was Liza's gasp of dismay that gave it

away. In her grief over Uncle Clark's death, she had forgotten the ruby atop her husband's dresser. Now, as if in a trance, she saw it before her, gleaming wickedly.

The policeman studied her intently. He had a satisfied smile on his face.

"I have the stone in my possession," Joseph said.

Bill looked astonished. The Inspector paused to clear his throat.

"And how did that happen?" Berthold asked.

"My Uncle gave me the ruby," Joseph said. "That was why he summoned me to his house yesterday."

Everyone stared at him. No one seemed to know quite what to say.

"He gave it to you," Berthold repeated. "Just — gave it to you?"

"I don't believe that," Bill cried, leaping to his feet.

"It is true, nonetheless," Joseph said, still quite calm.

"If I may be permitted," a voice said from the hall. They all turned toward it.

Again Al Zaghral had come in without Liza's knowing it. She had not heard the door, had not heard Mrs. Morgan — yet here he was, advancing into the room as if he belonged there.

"If I may be permitted," he said again, bowing around the room, "Mr. Hanson speaks the truth. I was present when the gift was made."

Joseph looked pleased with himself; the policemen looked disconcerted. Bill looked as if he would like to say something, but he thought better of it, and sat back down heavily.

There were a few more questions. Inspector Marks spoke for almost the first time, to ask if they knew of any enemies Mr. Rutherford might have had.

"He travelled extensively," Joseph said, "in some pretty wild places. God alone knows what enemies he might have picked up along the way."

At last they were gone. Bill left with them, muttering a hasty apology. Joseph seemed hardly to have minded his accusations.

Al Zaghral was the last to leave. Liza could not help but note that his manner with Joseph was oddly familiar as it had hitherto been with Uncle Clark — formal, and yet intimate, insinuating.

"That's one thing to be grateful for," Liza said when he too had gone. "We won't be seeing him in the future."

"I'm afraid we will," Joseph said. "I've asked him to stay on as my assistant."

"But why?" she asked, surprised.

"He's worked very closely with my uncle over the past few months," Joseph said. "There's many things he knows about the business, especially the new investments, that I don't know. I'm afraid I'd be rather lost without him, you see."

Liza, who didn't think her husband would be lost without anyone, did not pursue the matter. If her husband thought he needed Al Zaghral, and if he did not mind the man's company, it was not her place to complain. Certainly, as she had admitted so often, she knew nothing about business affairs. And no doubt she was being unreasonable about the Oriental. There was nothing specific he had ever done that she could complain of, nothing he had ever said to offend her. Indeed, in the matter of the Conners family he had been helpful to her, and just now it was his appearance that had saved Joseph from a difficult situation.

Remembering the policemen and their questions, she said, "Darling, about Bill, those things he said — you mustn't mind them. He was just upset, I'm sure when he's calmer he'll realize how foolish he sounded."

"You needn't worry about it," Joseph said. "In fact, you needn't worry about anything, my pet."

He put a finger under her chin and tilted it up, smiling down into her pretty face. "From now on, everything is going to be fine. Truly fine."

Chapter 5

A month later they moved into Sea Cliff.

It was not a move that particularly pleased Liza. She had a sort of grim respect for the house, but she could not imagine anyone really being comfortable or happy in the place.

One entered into a hall, at one end of which was a huge curved staircase with bare, stone treads and a wrought-iron banister. The walls were panelled, a dark and gloomy oak, and nearly one entire wall was a great open fireplace bristling with andirons and spits and tongs and even a huge cauldron. On the other walls were weapons, flintlocks and muskets, axes and swords and daggers.

Joseph, however, seemed pleased with the move, and in any event, he had not asked her what she thought, he had simply told her they were moving.

They had inherited Sea Cliff as well as the Rutherford Mills, and Clark Rutherford's other, newer investments. Joseph found some grounds for complaint in this re-

76

spect, however; Clark's sister Estelle, who had lived a number of years as a recluse, owned a share of Rutherford Mills. Additionally, Clark had left her part of his money, some more of the mills, and an interest in most of his investments.

"That old dragon," Joseph complained when the terms of the will were made known. "What can she possibly want with a share in the business?"

"What can it matter?" Liza asked, surprised at this callous attitude. "You've got the bulk of everything. You're running Rutherford Mills now. That was always what you wanted, wasn't it?"

"It's a nuisance, though, having another owner to satisfy. And you know what it's like to try to see her or talk to her. I'll spend half my time banging on her door, coaxing her to see me."

Aunt Estelle almost never saw anyone. Since her marriage, Liza had seen her only once, and then briefly. They had tacitly agreed to dislike one another, and there had never been occasion for another visit.

"I don't suppose she'll bother us," Liza said lamely.

"This house is a bother," Mrs. Morgan said when she had had her first good look at it. "Look at it, it's a monstrosity. How am I to take care of all this, I ask you? I've only got two hands and two feet, you know."

"I've got an idea," Liza said, brightening. "I was thinking about the Conners family — Mrs. Conners not really fit to work in the mill, and Glade too young to be working like that, and little Jessie — why don't I speak to Joseph about hiring them? There's plenty of room for them here, and they could all help you."

"Little ones, I expect in the long run I'd end up having to take care of them," Mrs. Morgan said. "Still, if they're used to helping out . . . it wouldn't hurt to give it a try, I suppose."

Joseph was reluctant at first. "We're moving up in the world, pet. We need servants, it's true, but what we need are trained domestics, someone who'll do us proud. These people are nothing but millhands."

"And we're nothing but mill*owners*," Liza reminded him.

In the end he gave his permission and Liza had only to convince the Conners. This, to her surprise, proved harder than convincing Joseph.

"I've never been nobody's servant," Mrs.

Conners said when the subject was broached with her.

"But you're only working for someone else, the same as you do in the mill," Liza argued. "And it would be much nicer, actually. You'd be working for a friend, just the three of you, and not with hundreds of others. And think how nice it would be for the children. There's plenty of room, you wouldn't all be crowded together, and Glade wouldn't have to work in a mill every day."

"Glade's a young man already," his mother said. "I don't reckon honest work will hurt him."

In the end it was the simplest argument of all that won the day. "I really do need you," Liza said, all but despairing of ever convincing the other woman.

Mrs. Conners looked steadily back at her. She had no answer to that. From the day that Liza had come to the door bearing books and a doll she, all of them, had been obligated to her. It was something Mrs. Conners had never intended, never wanted; all her life she had resisted being obligated to anyone. She knew what it meant, never feeling that you were quite as good, never quite able to call your soul your own. For a moment, for just a very brief moment, she had hated that soft-voiced creature in velvet and fur who had come to her door, threatening to destroy the tenuous security of her existence.

And yet, there had been the doll. How could she have ignored the light that flashed in Jessie's eyes when she saw the doll? Oh God, she did not have it in her to take that from her little girl.

And later, she had found the books on the floor. How Glade did like his books! Young Glade, who worked so hard, and had so little pleasure. Had she the right to deny him that little bit of it; a few books to read, a few evenings, perhaps a week or more, of escaping from life's drabness into that other world that he sometimes shared with her?

And that woman's soft but determined kindness, when kindness was long a stranger to her? Something in her heart wouldn't let her refuse that either.

So she had accepted — tacitly, by default, perhaps, but she had accepted the gifts. The doll had stayed, had taken a place of honor on Jessie's pillow. The books had been discovered, had produced — oh, that was almost reward enough — that gentle, deep smile of Glade's. And they had not been forced to move.

And now, when that woman sat across from her, and asked her to come to her house and be her servant, and put it that she needed her, she hadn't the right anymore to refuse, had she?

It was like she'd always said, once you were obligated, your soul wasn't your own anymore.

Jessie loved it, of course. There was the big lawn, hemmed in by wrought-iron fencing, for her to play in. There was the big nursery room for the children Clark's wife had never had, and more rooms than she could count for exploring.

Glade observed everything solemnly and without comment, but his eyes lighted up when he saw the library with its walls of leather-bound volumes.

"You must make free use of the books," Liza told him, and was gratified by the look of pleasure that flitted across his too-old face.

Mrs. Conners looked with mixed feelings at the huge suite of rooms that had been prepared for them. They were beautiful, of course, and promised a luxury of which she had never dared dream. There was even her own fireplace and the prospect, for the first time in her life, of being warm enough all the time.

She sighed; there was nothing to do but make the best of it. The children would be happier here. Jessie was already delighted, and Glade would come around to it. The dog, Erasmus, had already adopted Glade.

"He shall be your first responsibility, then," Liza said, and Glade had solemnly knelt down and patted the dog's head, sending Erasmus into paroxysms of ecstasy.

Yes, they would be happier in the long run. It was something else to be grateful for.

The presence of the Conners family in the house made Joseph unhappy. It was not, as he had argued with Liza, that they were inexperienced as domestic servants; he had no great respect for the art of domestic servitude, and certainly they were all smart enough, even the little girl, to learn.

No, it was the look on Mrs. Conners face — innocent, pure, and chronically apprehensive. Life had not been gentle to her; you would have expected that to make her bitter, but it had somehow left her compassionate, her innocence untouched. She was the sort of woman who would remain ignorant of self-pity, but would mourn the hardships of others.

Probably her intelligence was slight, and her faith great, and unquestioning. He could imagine her at night, praying for not only her family, but for everyone whom her mind had brushed, mothlike, for an instant.

He would have despised her utterly if he had been able to. He was awed by her, by her unshakable simplicity, by her patience and sincerity. She had in her eyes a far-distant look of one who has suffered unspeakable pain, and accepted it. Her innocence remained, but it was brutalized. It left that anxious look in her faded grey eyes, her nervous smile, intended to placate — to placate whom? God?

And she was spotless. Her dress was ancient and threadbare, but it was spotless, and she wore an apron of almost unbearable whiteness.

She reminded him of a starved animal, and when she waited upon him he saw that her hands were burnt with homemade soap and hard work at home and in the mills. Those hands seemed to him an accusation, a penance.

He had long ago lost his own innocence, and this was no doubt one reason for his resentment. But her age awed him, too, for she was older than he, and age always intimidated him somewhat. After all, had not the old suffered life's evil? Had not they learned the secret of endurance? And were they not brave, to live with being old?

So when she came to him and said, "I heard you coughing last night," he did not snap at her as was his inclination, but managed a barely civil nod.

"I have a syrup," she went on, and he could not say if she knew how he felt about her, or if she minded it; her face was impassive, beyond hurting. "It was my mother's medicine for a cough, and I give it to the children whenever they've got a cold. I would be glad to have you take some."

She saw the resentment in his eyes, and expected him to refuse, for she knew him as a man remote, as far from others as a tower on a hill. Still, she held out the bottle for him to take it.

He tightened his mouth, and saw her eyes, watery and shrinking, upon him. He wondered suspiciously what was in the medicine.

"It isn't good to suspect everyone," his mother used to tell him. "Imagine what the world would be like if no one trusted anyone else?"

Safer, he had thought. He reached for the syrup, taking it from her. She folded her wounded hands and put them under her apron, and did not seem to mind that he did not thank her.

Chapter 6

By all rights, Liza told herself again and again, she ought to be quite happy.

In the first place, they were rich, rich beyond her ability to grasp it, rich beyond her first realization of their wealth.

They lived at Sea Cliff, and if it was grotesque, it was equally grand. What's more, it was run with an almost alarming efficiency. Mrs. Morgan, of course, had always been a first rate housekeeper, but now she was aided by the Conners brood.

"And I've never seen people work like they do," she said. "Never talk, never complain, never laugh either, but they get it done, quick and right. They could teach lessons to a few house maids I've known, if you want to know."

Mrs. Conners, it sometimes seemed, was everywhere. You could hardly think of something you needed, or something you wished done, that she hadn't anticipated, and just as you were turning around to ring for her, there she was at your elbow, with whatever it was you wanted. She never questioned, never argued — hardly ever spoke except to answer directly a question you had put to her. She cooked when Mrs. Morgan didn't "get around" to it; she cleaned, she served, she sewed; she was an army of domestic servants in one.

Glade was her wraithlike helper, handing her dishes when she served, taking them from her as she washed. When there were chores to be done, wood to be cut or brought in, windows to be washed, rugs to be beaten, Glade did them silently and swiftly. Liza sometimes worried that the boy seemed never to enjoy himself, but then from time to time she would discover an empty space in the row of books in the library, and she would know that he had silently taken his own reward, and she would be pleased.

Even little Jessie worked, but she at least seemed to enjoy herself more than the others. One could often hear her little voice singing merrily as she helped in the kitchen, or see her hopping on one foot as she dusted.

Liza could not but think she had made a wise suggestion when she had asked to have the Conners family hired.

Everything seemed to be going beautifully, and yet she was unhappy. Part of the fault she could name easily — Al Zaghral. That man had become her husband's nearly full-time companion. Only at night, in the privacy of their bedroom, was she alone with Joseph. At other times the Oriental was with him, always smiling, always soft-voiced, always deferential — and yet she had the odd impression, which she would voice to no one, that Al Zaghral was the master, and Joseph the servant. And looking back, she found that she had had that same impression, not yet formed into words, with Uncle Clark.

Only once had she dared to voice a timid criticism of his constant presence. "Surely by this time you've learned all you need to know from him," she had said to Joseph.

"He's invaluable to me," was all her husband had said.

Al Zaghral was not the entire problem, though. What was far more worrisome to Liza was that her husband had changed. She could not say just when, although in her own mind she dated it from Uncle Clark's death. Nor could she analyze in detail just how he had changed: he was less gentle, less kind, less thoughtful, yet she could not say exactly when he had been anything but gentle or kind to her — certainly he had been generous to a fault. She had only to mention something she liked, something she desired, and it was hers at once.

At first it was only things he said, chance remarks he made, that bothered her. She remembered a conversation in which he had remarked that he intended to get far richer than he was.

"The best way to acquire wealth," he said, "is through politics."

Surprised, she said, "I had no idea you were interested in politics. Joseph, don't tell me you're considering running for office?"

"Me? No, hardly, that's too dirty for me," he said. "Far better to control the politicians. You find the skeleton in a man's closet, or his weakness, or his vice — every man's got one. Do him favors, but make him repay them. That's the way it's done."

He laughed, and after a moment she had smiled, too, as if he had been joking, but afterward, she had not been so sure.

Most puzzling of all was the ruby. In the past, Joseph had appreciated things for their beauty or their utility, but he had never been greatly attached to things. But it was as if the ruby obsessed him, almost as if he worshipped it. He had even created an altar for it. The little room off Clark's bedroom that had once been a reading room for him had been cleared of its furnishings. The walls had been draped in a deep velvet that also covered the windows, so that only a faint trickle of light filtered in.

In the center of the room, seeming to create its own light, the ruby sat in a glass box atop a marble pedestal. It was the focal point of the room; your eyes went to it the moment you entered, and you felt as if you could not look away from it. Its light drew you closer, held you spellbound. You seemed to feel, as you gazed into its blood-colored depths, that if you looked long enough, deep enough, you could see the answer to everything, the end-all, the essence of life. If you stared long enough, you might have an odd sensation of falling into those glowing depths, of drowning in ruby red.

The gem frightened her, she did not know why. It seemed to mock her, and she was not comfortable in the room with it. She sensed that somehow it was a source of danger to her, and though she scoffed at her fears, they remained.

At times the stone seemed to glow a deeper red, until it looked literally the color of blood, so real that you felt it must begin to flow down the pedestal, to stain the floor. Then it caused a sick feeling in the pit of her stomach, and she would hurry from the room with one hand at her throat.

The stone became the focal point of her growing uneasiness. She took all of her worries, all of her unhappiness, and laid them at the foot of the pedestal. The stone seemed to wink at her, mocking her. She was afraid to look into the depths, afraid of the answer she might find.

It was Bill Whitney who first gave concrete form to her fears about the ruby. She had not seen him in several weeks, but from Joseph's comments, and his own activities, she assumed Bill was extremely busy. The mill had continued to expand and, although she knew little enough about it, she understood that Joseph was continuing, as Uncle Clark had, with numerous new investments.

"But we have so much money already," she remarked on one occasion. "Why should we need any more? Why can't you just take time to enjoy what we have?"

"Money is power," he said, "and there is never enough of that. Be content, pet, be content."

And why not take your own advice? she thought, but she held her tongue.

Until Bill came to see her.

"You've been such a stranger," she said, ushering him into the parlor. She was genuinely glad to see him; until then she had not been aware of how lonesome she had been. In the past she had spent most of her leisure with her husband. The few friends they had had somehow drifted away from them the last few months, without her quite realizing it had happened. She made a mental note that they must plan a dinner party; she had suggested that before, when they had first moved into Sea Cliff, and Joseph had said no.

"We're not settled in yet," he had said. But surely that excuse was no longer valid. She would ask him again. In the meantime, it was good to see a friendly face; for the moment, she could even forgive Bill his romantic interest in her, although to tell the truth he did not seem very romantic just now.

"Where's Joseph?" he asked, hardly answering her greeting at all. He looked worried and, she thought, angry. He was not at all the relaxed, happy person she remembered.

"Why, I thought he was at the mill . . .

he's with that — with his assistant," she said.

"Isn't he always?" Bill commented drily. His glance went around the room; he seemed to be weighing something, and finding it wanting. "You're living well these days, Liza." The remark had a cutting edge to it, as if he did not approve of the fact.

"Yes, I must admit that we are," she said, puzzled. For a moment he stared at her, and it was such a disapproving look that she did not know what to make of it. "Is something wrong?" she asked. "Because we're living well? Aren't you? Bill, have you come here to ask for a raise? Because if you have, I'll be glad to put in a word with Joseph, if that's what you want."

"Do you think I would accept that kind of money?" Bill asked angrily. "Blood money, Liza?"

"Bill, I —"

"Do you know what these are?" he demanded, interrupting her. He took a sheaf of papers from his breast pocket and waved them under her nose. "These are men's lives, Liza, the lives of decent, honest men, maybe not as rich and powerful as your husband, but good, God-fearing men."

"I don't understand what you're talking

about," she said, taking a step back from him. "What men? What lives, for Heaven's sake?"

He flung the papers on a table. A single sheet fluttered to the floor and lay there, unretrieved.

"I'm talking about your husband's business activities," he said. "Those are the papers on two companies he just took over. He didn't just buy the companies from those men, he stole them, he tricked them, and squeezed them and backed them into corners he had created and then he took their businesses from them, their lifeblood. Jacob Farley, he was one of the men, and a good friend — he killed himself, Liza, because of what Joseph did to him."

"Bill, I'm sorry," she said, putting a tentative hand upon his shoulder. He hardly seemed to notice the gesture.

"And Jim Cooper, he's out in the streets, he's destitute. Joseph didn't even leave him a little dignity, a shred of pride. He's a ruined man. His life work has been taken from him."

"I'm sure Joseph didn't mean to ruin anyone," Liza said. "Perhaps if you spoke to him about your friend, Mr. Farley, wasn't it, he —"

"They aren't the only two. The files in Joseph's office are filled with cases like these. He's a monster, he's destroying men's lives, and he doesn't care."

A shudder went through Liza, but she drew herself up indignantly and said, "I must remind you, Bill, that you are speaking of my husband."

"He isn't your husband anymore, nor my friend," Bill said, "He's a monster, exactly like Clark Rutherford."

"How can you say that?" she cried, truly angry now. "Uncle Clark did everything for you, as well as for us. He was generosity itself, he was kind and gentle and good, as good a man as I've known."

Bill looked her squarely in the eye; he did not seem to notice her anger. *"Was,"* he said emphatically. "Yes, Liza, he was. But not at the end, not in the last few months of his life. He had become a monster, too, can't you see that?"

"I . . ." she said, and stopped. Her mind flashed back to her last meeting with Uncle Clark about the housing for the Conners. She thought of how he had changed, of his rudeness, of his coldness to her pleas for compassion.

"What are you trying to say?" she asked in a small, frightened voice.

He came toward her, seizing her shoulders as if he would shake her.

"The ruby," he said in a low voice. "Can't you see it for yourself, it's that blasted ruby."

"The ruby? What do you mean?" she asked. She had never seen Bill like this; she was as frightened of him as she was of what he was trying to say.

"That's what's done it," he said. "The curse on that stone, it changed them both. Clark changed the day he acquired that ruby — he got what he wanted, wealth and power, but it was like he'd sold his soul to the devil. And before he died, he gave it to Joseph, and Joseph has changed just as Clark did. Have you looked at your husband lately, Liza? Look at his face, it's lined like a man ten years older. You can see him changing almost before your eyes. He's gotten a hard, cruel look."

She hadn't seen any change, not consciously, and yet now that he made the remark, she seemed to see Joseph's face before her, and it was changed, subtle little changes, too small to be noticed day by day.

The thought frightened her still more, and her fear translated itself into anger. She thrust Bill's hands roughly from her, and moved away from him.

"I won't listen to any more of this," she said angrily. "I don't know if you've been drinking or what, but you're acting like a madman. I think you had better go."

He laughed drily. "So, you won't listen, you won't believe," he said. "Very well, that's your choice, but I warn you, you aren't living with Joseph anymore, you're living with a demon that's taken over his body and his soul. He's destroying people, everyone he comes into contact with, and mark my words, he'll destroy even you if you let him."

She was too distraught to make an answer to this, but it didn't matter, for he didn't wait to hear one. He seized up the papers he had brought with them, stuffing them haphazardly into his pockets. He whirled about and strode from the room, leaving her to stare bewildered after him. She heard the door open and then slam shut behind him.

"Mercy," Mrs. Morgan said, appearing in the doorway. "What got into him?"

"He . . . was in a hurry," Liza said.

Mrs. Morgan gave her a shrewd look. "Are you all right? You look fit to be tied yourself."

"Yes, I'm all right, thank you," Liza said,

hardly thinking what she was saying. In her mind she was going over the conversation she had just had.

Her thoughts kept coming back to the ruby. One thing that Bill had said was certainly true — the ruby changed men. Clark Rutherford had changed from the day he brought the stone home, and Joseph too had begun to change when he inherited the ruby. Perhaps it was cursed, that gem, cursed in the way it affected men's thinking.

As if drawn by a siren's call, Liza left the parlor and made her way up the wide stairs to the room in which the ruby was kept.

Sometimes the door was locked, but today it was not. It was as if she were expected, as if she had an appointment to see the stone.

It sat on its pedestal, gleaming. She stood before it and gazed into its depths, the color of blood. Blood . . . blood money, Bill had used that phrase. A blood ruby, Joseph had told her that was what the stone was called. A blood curse on it, Clark had said when he first showed it to them. Blood. Blood. *Blood.*

And now the stone gleamed darker, redder than ever, it seemed to her. It was as if it had absorbed the blood of the man who had just died, the blood of those whose lives were being trampled beneath Joseph's vaulting ambition for wealth and power.

That's impossible, she told herself. A stone did not change colors, it was only a trick of the light and her imagination, fired by Bill Whitney's crazy accusations.

And yet, was Bill crazy? She had known him for several years, she couldn't think of a saner, more sensible man in every respect but one — his infatuation with her. He was sensible to the point of dullness. He was not a man to believe in curses, in evil magic, surely.

She shook her head, trying to clear her thoughts. It was madness to accuse an inanimate object, a gem, however precious, of changing someone like Uncle Clark or Joseph into another person. As if the curse were real, as if such things existed. Joseph had gotten a taste of wealth and power, that was all; in time he would regain his equilibrium. And Uncle Clark — it was mere chance that his fortunes had changed just at the time he acquired the ruby.

And the ruby had not changed colors, it was only her imagination.

And yet . . .

She shuddered and turned from the stone, hurrying from the room.

Chapter 7

She found her husband in the corridor outside. He greeted her with a kiss, but she
could not bring herself to put her lips to his.
She turned away, and his kiss landed on her
cheek instead.

"Is anything wrong?" he asked, turning
her face so that he could look at her.

"No," she said, and then quickly, "Yes."
She leaned her cheek against his strong
chest, and closed her eyes. When she had
looked at his face, she had seen the
changes Bill had spoken of.

Surely, she thought, it is the power of
suggestion, nothing more. This is my Joseph, my husband, whom I love, whom I
have loved for years. Still, the lines were
there, and they haunted her.

"I just saw Whitney driving away as I
came up," he said. "This doesn't have
something to do with his visit, does it?"

She nodded wordlessly, still clinging to
him with a desperate fervor.

"I suppose he's been confessing his love
for you," Joseph said drily. Then, suddenly

he said, "Say, he didn't try to touch you, did he?"

"No," she said quickly, too quickly. She looked up at him searchingly. "He said you were a monster," she said.

For a moment he looked startled by the remark. Then, unexpectedly, he threw back his head and laughed.

"A monster, am I?" he said. "What else did he say, this is most interesting."

"Joseph, it isn't funny," she said, angered by his flippant attitude. "He said you're making your fortune on the blood of other men. A man named Jacob Farley, he killed himself because you took over his business; and another man, Jim Cooper, he's out in the streets because . . . well, because you took over his business, too, and . . ."

She stopped, intimidated by his look of amusement; even to her own ears, put like this, the charges sounded wild and a trifle foolish.

"Darling," Joseph said, speaking as one would speak to a difficult child, "This Mr. Farley you're speaking of, it's true, he did kill himself, but not because I took his business over. He killed himself because he ruined his business, he drove it into the ground. If I hadn't bought him out, someone else would have, don't you see?

He was broke, finished, whether I entered the picture or not. And as for Jim Cooper, yes, I bought him out, too, and he's out of a job, if you want to look at it that way — or he's retired, if you look at it the way I do. Now, what else did Mr. Whitney have to say about me?"

"Nothing," she said in an ashamed little voice.

"Come on, let's have it," he said. "Did he say I was attacking innocent maidens on the street? Selling babies to the heathens?"

She smiled timidly and said, "He said that you had changed. He said there was a curse on . . . on that ruby, and it had changed you."

He burst out laughing again, to her annoyance. "I don't think —" she said.

"Look, darling," he said hugging her tightly. "I'm sorry, but you've got to admit — the ruby has changed me into a monster, I'm squeezing all these helpless men out of their businesses, leaving them on the streets — it's like a Mrs. Radcliffe novel! You can't expect me not to laugh, now honestly, can you?"

He spoke so earnestly, held her so tightly to him, that she could not restrain a smile of her own. "I suppose you're right," she said.

"Of course I am." This time when he kissed her she did not turn away.

It was only the following day that the doubts returned.

It was Mrs. Conners's free day and she had gone out for the morning. It was lunch time when she returned, and Liza chanced to be coming down the stairs just as the other woman let herself in. She saw that Mrs. Conners looked particularly unhappy and preoccupied with something.

"Is anything wrong?" she asked.

Mrs. Conners paused in taking off her coat and hat and turned toward her. "Mrs. Hanson," she said, "I think that I must ask you to let me resign."

Liza was taken aback. "But . . . what has happened?" she asked. "I thought you were happy here, and certainly we have been happy with all of you."

"It's just, I can't work for people who . . ." She paused, embarrassed by her own temerity. "Mrs. Hanson," she said, a pleading note in her voice, "those people at the mill, I know a lot of them, some of them are my friends. Do you think I can work up here, all comfortable-like, and ignore the way things are with them? It makes a body feel like a traitor, can't you see?"

103

"I don't understand," Liza said, giving her head a shake. "The people at the mill — what have they got to do with anything?"

Mrs. Connors regarded her for a solemn moment. "Haven't you been down there lately?"

"No," Liza said.

"I just thought . . . well, you paid so much attention to us, I just thought you went down there regularly. I thought you noticed things . . ." Her voice trailed off lamely. She looked sorry to have broached the subject at all.

"Mrs. Conners," Liza said, "Is something wrong down at the mill?"

Mrs. Conners drew herself up, her pride reasserting itself. She had said too much already, she thought. "I'm sorry if I spoke out of turn," she said. "You've been most kind to us, I'm sure."

"There's no need to apologize, I assure you, but you must promise me that you will stay on here. We do need you, you know."

Mrs. Conners considered for a long moment before saying, "We'll stay on."

But when Liza tried to return to the subject of the millworkers, Mrs. Conners withdrew behind her curtain of reserve.

"I'm sure it's not my place to judge," was all she said before making her way up to her own room.

Her remarks stayed with Liza. She could not understand what had upset her. It was true, the life of the millworkers was a hard one, but that had always been so. At Rutherford Mills the workers had things better than at other mills, as Mrs. Conners should know.

But perhaps there had been changes. Liza had not been to the mills since Mrs. Conners and her family had come to Sea Cliff. So much had changed — Joseph was so very busy now, and she understood that the mills represented now only a small part of his interests.

She toyed with the idea of driving to the mills to see for herself what had upset Mrs. Conners so. She hesitated, but now curiosity won out; and she called for the carriage to be brought around, and was soon on her way across town.

She did not go into the offices but, leaving the carriage, went directly to the streets of houses belonging to the millworkers.

At first she could see nothing significantly different. The same plain houses stretched in rows along the muddy street. Yes, it lacked comfort and dignity, but it was the milltown Mrs. Conners was used to. Why should it suddenly perturb her now?

But when she came to the end of the street, she saw a new sight; where the houses ended, the settlement had been extended. Before there had been an open field there which had provided a crude playground for the local children. Now the entire area was filled up with housing — she had forgotten that Bill had told her before that the mills had had to hire a great many new workers, and of course they would need housing, too.

But to call these structures housing was to take liberties with the term. At least the others had four walls and a roof; they were reasonably solid, reasonably warm, adequate if not luxurious.

Now before her lay a field of lean-tos, shanties of the most wretched description. Many of them were open in front to the weather, and none looked as if they could withstand a good windstorm. They were without adequate ventilation and many had no means of heating apparent.

She could not believe that any people could live in such squalor, let alone workers for the Rutherford Mills. It was a disgrace to the name, an insult to the sensibilities.

She turned and made her way hurriedly back toward the mills, hardly noticing that she splattered her lovely skirt and her new shoes with mud and other filth. She could well understand now how Mrs. Conners had felt and why she had said she could not work for them without feeling like a traitor.

At the office she was disappointed to find Joseph was out. A new clerk, whom she did not know, studied her with frank curiosity.

"I'll see Mr. Whitney, then," she said lamely. She did not know what good that would do, but perhaps he could tell her something that would put her mind at ease. Perhaps those horrid dwellings she had seen were only temporary and were already being replaced by more solid structures.

"Sorry," the clerk said. "Mr. Whitney is no longer with the company."

"Bill?" she said, surprised. "When did he resign?"

The man smirked and said, "Well, he didn't exactly resign, he was thrown out, you see, yesterday, it was. Don't know myself just what it was all about, but it must have been something good. You see —"

But she did not wait to hear the rest. She

returned to her carriage slightly dazed. Bill, fired? He had been with Rutherford Mills for years, virtually all of his adult life — the mills *were* his life. Since before she had married Joseph, Bill had managed the office, had been a close advisor, had made himself seemingly indispensable in a thousand little ways.

Surely he had not been fired for the remarks he had made to her? There must be some other explanation, some reason unknown to her.

Or else *she* had contributed to his dismissal.

Joseph did not come home for dinner. She ate alone, picking at her food. Once or twice Mrs. Conners, who served the dinner, seemed on the verge of speaking to her, but held her tongue.

Nine o'clock came and still Joseph had not come home. She waited up until ten, and at last, feeling unspeakably weary, she went up to bed.

She was just brushing her hair out when at last Joseph arrived. He seemed mildly surprised to see her still up. He came to her and bending down kissed the back of her neck.

"Joseph," she said, looking at his reflection in her dressing-table mirror, "why did you fire Bill?"

"Who says that I did?" he asked.

"I was told he was fired. No one else would do that, no one would dare without your instructions."

He shrugged and straightened up. "Very well, if you must know, I did fire him. I didn't think you concerned yourself with business matters, my dear."

"But why did you?" she insisted.

"Because he had become a nuisance. Do you need to ask me why, after his visit here yesterday?"

"But to fire him!" she said. "Oh, yes, I can see that you might be angry, I can agree that he was rude, that he showed poor judgment, even. But surely it was not necessary to fire him. Surely a chastisement would have sufficed."

"Darling," he said, kneeling beside her. He put his arms about her, and the fingers of one hand toyed with her dark hair. "Why do you fret so about things that don't concern you? I fired Bill Whitney because I could no longer trust him to work for my best interests and not against me. Bill was intimately concerned in almost all of my interests. He made it plain that he disliked working for me, he disliked many of those interests, he even disliked me. How could I have had the confidence in him that I needed? Can you not see my position?"

"I suppose so," she said lamely. What he said made sense, so far as she could judge. And yet, it was still not fair, to her way of thinking.

"You needn't worry about Bill," he said, kissing her neck again. "I made him a generous settlement. I assure you he's not destitute. Does that relieve your mind?"

"Oh, darling, yes, it does," she said, turning to return his kiss. It was a relief to know that Bill would not be in straits as a result of all this.

"And now," Joseph said, drawing her into an embrace, "can we consider the subject closed?"

"I suppose so," she murmured.

"Then, as long as you are still awake . . ."

She woke late to find him already gone. She stretched catlike, staring reflectively up at the ceiling.

How different it had been! Not like Joseph at all. She knew little enough about such things, Heaven knew, but she had always considered herself fortunate that Joseph was the lover he was. She had heard other wives talk, and she had an impression that men in general were bestial in their lovemaking, while Joseph had always been gentleness itself, undemanding, considerate . . .

But last night he had been another man altogether, wild, brutal even.

She got up and went to her dressing table. Her lips seemed to burn still from his kisses. There was a bruise on one shoulder, and a mark on her throat where he had kissed her.

She touched the bruise gingerly with one finger, and stared at her reflection, and wondered.

Chapter 8

She made an effort to see Bill. She knew where he roomed and the following day, without saying anything to her husband, she drove there. She did not know herself exactly why, except that she had a feeling it was important to have Bill know he was not fired because of her.

The landlady of the boarding house was a round-faced woman beyond middle years whose hard, calculating eyes belied her almost constant smile.

"I'd like to see Mr. Whitney," Liza said, and the woman's smile faded briefly.

"I'm his employer's wife," she added quickly.

"Well, that's good to know, I must say," the woman said. "Never mind what I thought at first, you probably don't know what it's like trying to run a boarding house, I've seen some pretty funny goings-on in my day. Oh, not that anyone ever pulled anything here, I must say — I run a respectable place."

"And Mr. Whitney is a gentleman,"

Liza felt compelled to say.

"He is that," she said, the smile returning.

"Is he in?"

The landlady gave her round head a shake. "No, ma'am I can't say as he is. Begging your pardon, but did you say you are his employer's wife?" Liza nodded. "Funny, I thought I heard him say he was no longer employed."

The hard eyes studied her intently.

"Well, yes, he has just left our employ," Liza stammered. "That's what I wanted to talk to him about. Do you know when he'll return?"

"Well, I can't say as he will. It was my understanding he was moving out. Leastways, he paid his bill, and took his things with him."

Liza felt a sinking feeling in her stomach. "Did he say where he was going?" she asked.

"No, ma'am, he didn't."

"Well . . ." she said lamely, uncomfortable under the other woman's scrutiny. "Thank you."

She looked back as she drove away and saw that the landlady was still in the doorway, watching her.

So, Bill had gone. There was nothing

more she could do about him, and in any event, there was really no need for her to worry about it further. Joseph had assured her that he had taken care of Bill generously. Perhaps Bill had decided to use the money to settle somewhere else, or perhaps he was taking a much-needed vacation.

The thought that he had left without even saying good-bye weighed heavily upon her.

Estelle Rutherford lay late abed that morning. She was dreaming of Philip, a man she had loved once long ago and had planned to marry.

She hadn't married him, of course. She hadn't married anyone. Philip had been the one, and he had gone away to war and never come back, and she had closed off her house and her life and never given a thought to marrying anyone else — at least not until it was too late.

"Good-bye." She could hear his voice as clearly as if it were a moment ago. "Goodbye, my darling, don't worry, I'll come back to you."

It was spring and the air was thick with the perfume of apple blossoms. She breathed in deeply — and coughed herself painfully awake.

It wasn't spring at all, it was winter, and there were no blossoms, and there had been no Philip for more years than she could count.

She glanced at the wall and saw it was eleven o'clock by the old clock there. Blast that Phoebe, where was she? She never failed to wake her at seven when she brought in the tray.

She looked around, half-sitting up in the bed. The tray wasn't here, either. Blast her, this was really unconscionable. She reached for the bellrope and gave it a hearty tug. She could hear the chimes sounding far down in the depths of the house. There, that ought to bring her running with some trivial excuse. She sank back onto the pillow and closed her eyes.

Philip: she could all but hear the sound of his laughter. How he had liked to tease her! She remembered the hat she had worn that day. It was wide-brimmed, and the brim got narrower in front. There were flowers massed on top, and they fell across the front brim, hanging slightly over one eye.

"My little flower-maiden," he had called her, laughing, and she had blushed and grown angry because he teased her.

"This is what the smart ladies are

wearing in New York and Paris," she had told him sharply.

"And none so pretty in it as you," he said soberly, and he reached down and kissed first one eyelid and then the other, and then her lips . . .

Her eyes flew open. Had she dozed off? How long had it been since she rang for Phoebe? Where was she anyway? The house lay about her as still as a tomb.

A sudden thought chilled her. Suppose something had happened to Phoebe? She was no spring chicken herself, and she had a bad heart. What if she had died during the night?

The thought that she might be sharing a house with the presence of death really frightened the old woman. She reached for the bellpull again and tugged it furiously until the rope broke off in her hands. She fell back breathing loudly, her breath rattling ominously in her throat.

There was a noise outside. She cocked her head to one side and held her breath, straining to hear. There, she heard it again, something on the stairs.

She breathed a sigh of relief. Phoebe coming after all with the tray and the excuse.

"Well, she'll get a piece of my mind before I let her off the hook," Estelle said. She tried to plan just what she would say, but she was too relieved at discovering she was not alone in the house to really put her heart into a scolding.

There was another sound, at the top of the stairs this time, a curious, scraping sound.

She held her breath again and listened. Yes, there it was, coming closer, a shuffling sort of noise.

She frowned. It sounded nothing like Phoebe. Phoebe had been with her almost fifty years, and morning in, morning out, she had listened to the sound of Phoebe's footsteps in the hall. Well, she'd be hanged if this was Phoebe coming.

If not Phoebe, though, who? She sat up again, tugging the bedclothes up in front of her. Oh, Lord, she thought, and shivered, not a prowler, not one of those awful people that one read about so often these days. Maybe something had already happened to Phoebe, maybe . . .

It was closer now and still she could not identify the sound. It was a strange, scraping, shuffling sound, and blended with it something that sounded like many people whispering together.

Her heart began to hammer. She knew,

knew as surely as she knew her name, that this was nothing ordinary, nothing harmless. Something evil was out there, something evil had happened to Phoebe. She began to cry. She tried to pray, but she could not remember what came after *"Holy Mary, Mother of God."*

"I'll scream," she thought in a moment of resolution. "I'll run to the window and fling it open and scream."

But she didn't move. She knew she hadn't the strength to run across the room, let alone lift that window and scream.

Whatever was there had stopped outside her door, was just waiting there, as if it were torturing her by prolonging the agony.

She thought of the craziest thing then: when she had been little she had been plump. Not fat, but plump, with a round face and a squat, thick, little body. And when their parents died she had gone to live with her Aunt Clara, Clara Potter. She remembered as clearly as if it were yesterday going to a new school, and the children who hadn't liked her. She was shy, and plump, and she had just lost her parents.

"Piggy Potter," they used to call her, and when she would burst out crying and run from them, they would chase her and call her that over and over again.

"My name wasn't even Potter," the old woman thought, and she began to cry. She sat alone in her bed, huddled in her blankets, and cried, for the little girl she had been, and the old woman she was, both frightened.

The door crashed open then and her sobs caught in her throat. She stared and her fright became terror, a terror beyond screaming, beyond fleeing.

"Holy Mary," she began in a cracked voice — and mercifully she fainted.

"Mother of God," Inspector Marks murmured. His professional eye scanned the room, observing a myriad of details that a less-skilled observer might overlook: the broken bellpull, the arm that hung at an odd angle as if a mighty yank had pulled it from its socket, the marked wall where the door had been flung open with tremendous force.

"Ugly business, isn't it?" Inspector Berthold said. "These two old women weren't murdered, they were butchered."

"Robbery, do you suppose?" Marks was making notes in a little book that he carried with him.

Berthold looked at the gold candlesticks on the chest of drawers, the untouched jewel box at the vanity table. "No, not robbery, but that's not to say money didn't enter into it."

"Inheritance, maybe?" Marks glanced up from his writing.

"Didn't you get the old woman's name? Rutherford. You haven't forgotten that other one already, have you?"

"Rutherford! By God, you're right," Marks said, snapping his fingers. "That old geezer looked a lot like this, too, now that I think of it."

They left the bedroom and went down the narrow stairs; the house was filled with policemen measuring, marking, taking notes.

"I think we'll go see that young fellow again," Berthold said, leading the way. He paused at the front door.

"Have you noticed anything peculiar?" he asked.

"Not aside from the brutality of the murder." Marks looked puzzled.

"How did the murderer get in?"

"Why, he . . ." He paused and looked around. His puzzlement deepened.

"All the doors locked, bolted from the inside. Windows all closed and locked, no sign of anything broken or tampered with."

"They must have let him in themselves," Marks said.

"And bolted the doors after him?" Berthold asked. "And went back to their beds, and waited to be murdered?"

Marks, who saw that he had made a foolish suggestion, tried now to defend it. "It must have been something like that," he said, "unless you think some kind of ghost did it."

"Hummm, yes, a ghost," Berthold said, going out. "I'd almost be willing to believe it was something not human."

Chapter 9

Just a few days before, it had seemed to Liza that she was enjoying the essence of happiness — wealth, health, a husband who loved her, to lie in his arms, to trust in him to care for and protect her, to share to the fullest the richness of each and every moment.

But nothing could stand entirely alone. Not her love for Joseph nor any other part of her life nor moment of time could be isolated without reference to its juxtaposition with what had been before and what would be after. One's life at the beginning was flat and smooth, and as one progressed it took shape, the major events and concerns making peaks and valleys as they rose up around one. But the peaks and valleys formed a continuous line without breaks between them.

And even while she had thought herself happy, her life good, the very fibers of her life had been twisting into this new knot. A new tragedy had been patterned, at least in part from the materials of her life.

"How did Aunt Estelle die?" she asked

of the two policeman; she did not ask "How was she murdered?" deliberately, as if not mentioning the word could make the fact go away.

"Brutally," was the simple answer. Inspector Berthold added, "Like your uncle, Clark Rutherford."

Joseph said, "It was robbery, I suppose."

Liza gave him a sideways glance. He looked so pale and shaken that she could not but be a little puzzled. It was tragic, yes, this new death, and mysterious that murder should have entered their lives again like this; but he knew Aunt Estelle only slightly better than she did, as he had often told her. She could not have thought the old woman's death would matter particularly to him; yet he was deeply shaken, she knew him well enough to see that, despite his efforts to conceal his feelings. She saw it in the way his hand shook as he lighted a cigar, and in the urgency with which he poured himself a shot of whiskey and downed it.

"We rather think not," the Inspector replied.

"But surely," Joseph said. "Just the two of them, her and that old housekeeper, alone in that big house — she was known to have money, and there have always been stories that she kept large sums there in the house."

"I hadn't heard that," Marks said, making notes. "Did she?"

The Inspector looked up at him. "Did she keep large sums in the house?"

"How should I know?" Joseph said hastily.

"But you just said —"

"I said there have always been stories to that effect. I didn't really know her well enough to know if they were true. To be frank, we were not on the most intimate of terms. My aunt was a recluse. But surely you must know that already?"

The Inspector answered with another question. "By-the-by, when did you last see your aunt?"

Joseph, usually so calm, looked nonplussed. "Why . . . I can't even think, actually. It's been years, I suppose — wouldn't you say, darling?"

He looked to Liza for confirmation, but before she could answer, Inspector Berthold said, "As a matter of fact, you met with her a week ago yesterday, did you not?"

Joseph hesitated only a second or two before he said, "Yes, now that you mention it, I believe I did. It had quite slipped my mind."

Liza tried not to look surprised. Joseph had not mentioned seeing Aunt Estelle; she could not remember his having mentioned her at all since the reading of Uncle Clark's will.

"Would you mind telling me the nature of that visit?" Berthold asked.

"I would be very surprised if you did not already know the answer to that," Joseph returned a bit drily.

Unperturbed, Berthold said, "You went with your attorney. Documents were drawn up to insure that, in the event of her demise, the various businesses and investments would remain in family hands." He paused and added with emphasis, "Your hands, Mr. Hanson."

"Yes, that was essentially the nature of my visit," Joseph said.

"Those businesses and investments are considerable, are they not?"

"Yes," Joseph said.

"And yet this meeting quite slipped your mind?"

For a long moment the two men exchanged looks. Then Joseph said, "Quite."

Berthold closed the little notebook he had been consulting and returned it to his pocket. He stood up. As if on cue, his associate did likewise.

"I assume that you can account for your activities throughout the day yesterday," the Inspector said offhandedly.

"I have no doubt I can do so to your satisfaction," Joseph said.

"I don't know that it will satisfy me," Berthold said. "I don't know that at all, sir. Good-day. Mrs. Hanson."

Liza saw them to the door; she felt inadequate, as if there ought to be something she could say, something to add to the conversation that would prove Joseph quite innocent, or at the very least affirm her own belief in his innocence. But the words that she sought eluded her, and in the end she could only say lamely, "I hope you find the murderer."

He looked at her, she thought, with sympathy. Anger, accusation, coldness, these would have been easier to bear; sympathy was most disconcerting.

Joseph was having another drink when she returned to the parlor. He tipped his glass toward her and said, "I think that gentleman half-believes I killed Aunt Estelle."

The remark was followed by a silence. She did not know what to say. She was conscious of the ticking of the clock in the hall, and that Joseph was drinking rather heavily for so early in the day.

He looked at her at last and cocked one eyebrow. "Do you think so, too?"

"No, of course not," she said quickly. "Only . . . only I did wonder why you hadn't mentioned seeing her. It wasn't the usual thing, you have to admit."

"I didn't think about it," he said sullenly, downing the rest of his drink. "And if I had, I wouldn't have thought you'd be interested. You've never been interested in business matters before."

"Not in business matters, that's true. But Aunt Estelle, she was such a recluse, we've talked about her before. And to just go see her, it was so unusual —"

"Damn it," he said, putting his glass down with a bang. "I won't be cross-examined by my own wife."

She was so startled by the outburst that she could only stare wide-eyed as he went past her out of the room. She heard the door open, then slam shut after him.

She went into the empty hall and stared at the door as if it would open again and re-admit her husband; he would take her in his arms and laughingly apologize, and then he would explain away all the doubts and fears that were plaguing her, and peace and happiness would be restored in their home.

But the door stubbornly remained closed, and in her heart she knew that if Joseph did return the scene would not be played as she had imagined it.

She went up the stairs, as if drawn by an irresistible force, straight to the room in which the ruby was kept. She walked up to the pedestal and stared down through the glass at the stone.

Surely it was glowing redder than ever! She thought of the tragedies that had occurred — Uncle Clark's death, the people who had suffered as Joseph's wealth increased, Aunt Estelle's death. It seemed to her that the ruby was feeding upon the blood of its victims — *Joseph's* victims, for if they were victims, their deaths were at his feet in a sense. He had profited from each death, each tragedy.

She left the ruby and tried to leave behind her disquieting thoughts. She went to her own room, and stood at the window. From there she could see the cliffs beyond the house which gave the place its name. Far below the ocean's waves pounded with unceasing fury upon the jagged rocks rimming the beach. Even from there she could hear their roar, muted, but angry and threatening nevertheless.

Suddenly she knew it was true — the

curse, the awful legends, the evil that she had laughed at before. The stone *did* possess some magical and terrible power; it could bring one's wildest wishes true, wealth, power, no doubt almost anything one wished for.

And finally, perceived too late, she saw that the power that was meant to serve the ruby's owners in fact possessed them instead. It was they who became slaves to the stone's evil, to its curse.

Bill Whitney had been right, at least in part. Joseph had become, not a monster, but a slave to a monstrous power of evil. The man she loved, to whom she was married, was no longer the master of his own soul, of his life, of his actions.

But he was not a monster, no, she would never agree to that. She believed that if he could be freed from the stone, freed from the curse, he would still be her Joseph, the same man he had been before. He, the intrinsic person who was Joseph Hanson, had not changed; it was as if his personality had been overlaid by a pattern of evil.

Somehow, she thought, leaning her cheek against the cold glass, she must save him, she must free him.

But how?

Chapter 10

She had felt that she must go out into the snow-clad city, glittering in the sunshine with a gaiety that belied her own feeling of depression. She would go Christmas shopping. She ought to have started sooner, but somehow this year the holiday which ordinarily held such charm for her seemed flat and uninteresting.

She had come to bed late the night before, waiting up in the hope that Joseph would come in and they could set their quarrel to rights. At last, tired beyond the mere physical sense, she had given up and gone to bed. She had not even heard her husband come in, although she heard him preparing to leave in the morning. He went out without a word to her, and she had gotten up feeling drained, more exhausted than when she had retired.

She picked up the clothes that Joseph had scattered about the room when he came in the night before. They were new, part of the extensive new wardrobe he had lately purchased, but already they were redolent of his soap, of his tobacco, of his person. They had taken on creases from his body.

It gave her a sense of pleasure, of possession, to touch his clothes like this, to fold them away. Life must go on for them, it must be set aright. Things must never change.

But that thought brought back her unhappiness; things had changed, they had changed for the worse, and she must try to change them back again.

With these thoughts in her mind she had hurried into outdoor clothes and driven into the city. She dismissed the carriage and set out walking through the city's fashionable shopping streets.

She found herself, unexpectedly, in the street before the cathedral. People were hurrying toward it; a service was just beginning, she supposed. For a moment she almost entered the church herself, but restlessness drove her past it instead.

"What beautiful flowers," she thought, spying some in a window still half-clouded with morning frost. She engrossed herself in her shopping, admiring the window displays going from one to another, her face glowing from the cold. She was young, she was feminine, and she was out shopping.

For a time she all but forgot her troubles. The trees along the street sparkled in the snow, the buildings all looked doubly beautiful.

A trolley went by, the bells of the horses jingling. It stopped near her and she had an urge to get in it and let it take her where it chose. Perhaps it would carry her somewhere beyond fear, beyond worry.

But no, it would carry her beyond Joseph, too, and that would not do. She walked on. In the distance she heard voices singing *"Hark the Herald Angels sing, Glory to the newborn King!"* She hummed the tune to herself. The air was cold but exhilarating. The snow flew up in a dry powder at the touch of her feet. The wintry branches of the trees stood up like white coral.

She came to the edge of a park. Inside the little garden women were sweeping the paths clear of their late powdering of snow. In the stillness she could hear the voices of children playing. The air was so still that the slenderest twigs stood motionless, each one bearing upon itself its feathery burden of snow. Their pale tracery glittered against the blue of the sky. Brought to life by the burst of sunshine, starlings chattered in the evergreens. Now and then a bird would fly up into the open, making a little cloud of silver dust as the powdered, displaced snow hung for an instant in the sunlight.

Here in this magic garden it was almost warm. She brushed away the snow from one of the seats and sat down. Three pale, overdisciplined little boys in dark-green coats passed her, walking beside a fashionable governess. A young man, probably a student, went arm-in-arm with a young girl, both of them smiling as they walked. A soldier of some cavalry regiment turned to look at the young woman sitting unattended in the winter sunshine, and permitted himself the homage of a smile. She did not notice, and he passed on, his expression cool now and impersonal.

It was so beautiful here in this hushed garden; beautiful, far-away, unreal. She looked back over the nearly two years since Clark Rutherford had arrived home with his splendid new acquisition. She thought of Joseph, of the changes in him, so subtle at first that she hardly perceived them. She remembered her burst of possession this morning; something in her would snap if Joseph were taken from her.

Her husband. The impetuous yet oddly sensitive male creature who took her in his arms in the darkness, who was grateful to her for her womanness. From the first he had shown forbearance and great tenderness and out of these things her love for him had put forth a hot, Maytime bud and burst into full bloom.

A puff of wind brushed the garden, blowing the dry snow before it. She suddenly stood, so suddenly that she startled the starlings. She knew what she must do.

She must dispose of the ruby.

Chapter 11

All of her life she had been sheltered, protected; decisions had been made for her, first by her parents, later by her husband. In common with the women of her time she had led a passive life. She had never before had to think for herself, to make decisions, to take action. It was both frightening and exhilarating to suddenly be playing an active role.

Joseph was not at home; that undoubtedly meant that Al Zaghral was not there, either. She had been praying fervently for that kind of luck all the way home.

She saw no one when she came in. Mrs. Morgan was no doubt busy downstairs, Mrs. Conners would be helping in the kitchen at this time of day, and Glade would be running errands for her. Jessie spent this part of the day in her room playing.

Nothing could be simpler, really. She could not think why she had allowed the ruby to frighten her as it had all this time without taking action sooner. She had only to go to that room, remove it from its case, and . . . and *what?* she asked herself, pausing on the stairs.

She could sell it, no doubt — or give it away.

"No," she said to herself. "That would be to give away the curse as well. I couldn't inflict that on some other unsuspecting person."

"I'll throw it away," she said aloud in a sudden burst of resolution. She would take it to the cliff and fling the stone into the ocean. It would never be recovered from there, and the world would be well rid of its evil curse.

She hurried up the stairs to the room where the gem waited on its pedestal. She paused on the threshold, overcome by a sudden wave of fear and hesitation. Dared she go through with it? She suddenly thought of Joseph's reaction when he returned home and found the gem missing; would he thank her for her intervention, or would he curse her for a fool who had destroyed his wealth and power? She did not know, and not knowing frightened her more than the ruby itself or anything that had happened heretofore. Did she know her husband so little, then, that she was unable to guess how he would react?

136

The answer was Yes. Their conventions, their lives up to that point had in fact kept them strangers to one another. Neither of them had ever bothered before to try to get beneath the surface of the other, to try to learn what was behind the polite masks they had been taught to wear. They were husband and wife, they shared the ultimate physical intimacy, and yet their intimacy was no more than that total strangers might share in the night.

She shook her head forlornly. She must go through with this, whether Joseph thanked her or not; if a man were drowning and you tried to save him, he might strike at you, even push you away in his hysteria, but the obligation was there to try to save him anyway, despite himself.

She dared not let herself think of Al Zaghral's reaction to what she was going to do. She knew that his polite manners and his patronizing smile were only a thin veneer over an incredible evil.

She drew her shoulders back and entered the room, going directly to the pedestal. The glow of the stone seemed ominous, threatening, as if it knew her intentions. Her hand trembled as she reached for the glass case that covered the ruby. The glass was icy to her touch.

The glass did not move. She pulled at it and pushed it and tried to lift it, but it remained solidly in place. She ran her fingers around the edges, looking for a catch of some sort or other that held it, but she found nothing but the smooth edge. She knelt to examine it closer, but still she found nothing.

"Ridiculous," she told herself. "Something has to be holding it, there must be a way of taking the stone in and out."

But try as she would she could not find it. A sudden fury of frustration came over her and she began to hit the glass, pounding on it with her fists, but still it did not budge nor did it crack.

She was beside herself; it was like a contest of wills between the glass and herself. She looked wildly around the room seeking some weapon. There was nothing in sight.

She ran to her own room, looking there as well. Her glance fell upon a brass candlestick. She seized it at once and rushed back to the room in which the ruby waited.

She lifted the candlestick above the pedestal. And yet she hesitated. For a moment a feeling of dread overcame her, so that her hand trembled and she nearly lost her will to act.

"Curse you," she said aloud, and

brought the candlestick down on the glass. The glass case shattered, spewing splinters of glass about the room. Again she lifted the heavy brass stick and brought it down, and again, until only a few shards of glass remained where the case had been.

She brought her hands down and let the candlestick slip from her fingers. It fell to the floor with a thud. She stood looking down at the pedestal, panting with her exertion and the force of her emotion. There before her lay the ruby, defenseless, waiting to be seized, to be flung into the ocean's depths, never again to trouble her.

Still her hand did not move to seize it. She could not think what it was that held her back. It was only a gem, a piece of rock. She was alone there with it, it was too late now to turn back.

Slowly she reached out her hand toward the ruby. It seemed to her that the stone was even more frightening in its vulnerability. Some instinct within her seemed to warn her, even as she reached for it, that her victory would not, could not, be this simple.

"Don't touch that."

She gave a little cry of fright and whirled about, to find Al Zaghral there, virtually at her side. She had not heard him come in

139

from outside, she had heard no hurried footsteps on the stairs — yet there he was, breathing quickly as if he had just run up the stairs, as if the ruby itself had summoned him, had sent him some unheard distress signal.

His presence gave a concrete form to her fears, but pride gave her the courage to say "How dare you order me about? This is my home, that is my husband's property. I shall do with it as I wish."

He took a step closer to her and she shrank back from him, leaning across the pedestal itself. But he did not touch her. He smiled, showing his ugly, yellowed teeth; but his eyes did not smile. They gleamed with a fire that might have been reflected from the ruby, an evil glow that threatened wordlessly.

"I humbly beg your pardon," he said, making his little bow. "But I have been entrusted with the care of the stone. That is an office which I must carry out at any expense, even at the expense of your anger. I know that when you understand, you will forgive my presumption. And now, please. . . ."

He moved toward the pedestal. She hated herself for her cowardice, but she moved out of his way. She watched his long, narrow fingers close over the ruby, and knew that he had defeated her.

Angrily she said, "You won't stop me, you know. I'll find a time when you aren't here. You can't watch your precious stone all the time."

It was a direct challenge, and she was sorry at once that she had said it. But if it worried him, he did not show it in the least. He only smiled again, that loathsome, sneering smile, and with a last bow, walked from the room.

To add salt to her wounds, when he was in the hall, she heard him laugh — not a loud bellow of a laugh, but a low, mocking chuckle.

Chapter 12

She locked herself in her room, to which she had fled, and flung herself across her bed. She cried, as much from frustration as from fear or disappointment. From tears she slipped into sleep, a sleep troubled by dreams of the ruby and of Al Zaghral; her unconscious mind confused one with the other so that they became, not two separate entities, but differing aspects of the same entity, as a coin has two sides.

She was awakened by the sound of carriage wheels in the drive and ran to the window in time to see her husband return home.

This was the moment she dreaded most, when she must face Joseph. There was no way to excuse her actions, no foolish explanation that would make them seem trivial and harmless. Even were Al Zaghral not there to tell him, with what embellishments she could hardly imagine, he had only to go into that room and see the glass broken upon the floor to know. She was a fool to have given vent to her anger that way. Common sense alone told her there was some way to open that case, that might have given her now some avenue of escape from her dilemma. Without the broken glass, that evil man could have accused her of anything, but there would have been no proof.

Still sniffling, she went to the door and leaned her ear against it, listening. She could hear nothing, actually — an occasional muffled sound that might be a footstep, a distant murmur that was either voices or the echo of the sea. No doubt they were together, Al Zaghral talking in that oily-smooth voice of his, Joseph listening with a frown on his face, occasionally nodding his head.

At last she heard a sound that made her heart skip a beat — it was the sound of Joseph's footsteps in the corridor, coming closer. She moved quickly back from the door, facing it with eyes wide. She held a handkerchief in one hand; without knowing it she had already twisted it into knots.

The door opened. Joseph came in. He glanced at her, but with indifference. He closed the door after himself and crossed to the mirror, pausing before it to straighten his cravat.

She could not take her eyes from him. She stared at the back of his head, at his reflection in the mirror, at the deftness with which his fingers adjusted the twist of cloth.

At last he turned to her. She braced herself for the anger she was sure was coming. Her mind fought frantically for some words with which to defend herself.

"I've come up to tell you I shall not be home for dinner," he said. "I've a business deal to close. It may keep me late."

It was so totally unlike what she had expected that it left her speechless. She stared dumbly at him, but he had nothing further to say. He tilted his head slightly, his glance only just sliding off her, and he went out.

A shudder went through her as the door closed again. This was worse, far worse, than outspoken anger. His feelings went beyond anger. She knew him well enough to know that there was a point beyond which his anger did not travel, a point beyond which he was only capable of detestation so deep that it need not, could not, be expressed.

Again she burst into tears. She wished now that she had been the one to broach the subject. She wished she had thrown herself at his feet and pleaded forgiveness for her impetuosity. So many times before she had done foolish, thoughtless things, and he had never failed to forgive her. He was a generous, a magnanimous husband, he had always been so.

But when her fit of crying had passed, her feelings again changed to anger. She rubbed her hand across her eyes, little caring how it reddened them, and lashed out in silent anger at the two of them.

This was infamous! How dare he treat her so callously, with such indifference, as if she did not matter, as if her feelings were of no importance. Was her anger, her action, so trivial, of so little consequence, then? She pictured Al Zaghral, she imagined the smooth way in which he had told Joseph of the scene between them. Had they laughed at her, dismissing her as a foolish, childish wife?

Never had Joseph failed in any way to notice her unhappiness or her anger, never, until this day. She had been frightened before, even angry, that Al Zaghral had come between Joseph and his sense of honor. Without understanding it, she knew that it was an evil situation.

But now he had come between Joseph and herself, and that was beyond endurance. She felt as if she had been given a slap in the face.

Very well then, she would accept the challenge. Let it be war.

But if it was war, it was an uneven battle from the beginning. In the face of her husband's chilling indifference, she was more than willing to try again to dispose of the ruby; indeed, she now regarded it as absolutely necessary if she was to save her marriage. But try though she might, she was unable to gain access to the ruby without at once finding herself in the company of the man she despised most in the world, Al Zaghral.

It was as if he had some sixth sense that warned him whenever she was near the stone. No matter where he was, no matter how far, he was instantly on hand, as if carried on the wings of demons.

She tried time and again. She went to that damnable room at midday, when both men were out, only to be followed in by Al Zaghral. She feigned sleep at night and in the darkest hours she would creep from her bed, steal along the corridors and into the room where the ruby waited — only to be greeted by a smile and a courteous bow from its guardian.

She was beside herself with frustration. She grew nervous and irritable, she could not sleep well, and she lost her appetite. She became almost frantic in her efforts. It was now the *raison d'être* of her existence, to be alone with that stone.

Every effort was met with failure. What was even worse, though, was that neither the Oriental nor Joseph seemed in the least concerned. There was no doubt that they had marked her efforts, and it seemed to her as if they watched her with amusement. This fact drove her almost wild with anger and humiliation, but to no avail. The ruby remained where it was, untouched by her hands, guarded day and night as if by magic.

And then at last, it seemed as if the golden opportunity had presented itself. Joseph had again informed her that he would be late at his club with business associates.

She said, an idea already forming in her mind, "Will your assistant be with you?"

He asked, "Why do you want to know?"

She faced him directly and said, "Because he makes me uncomfortable. I do not like to be in the house alone with him."

"You would hardly be alone in any event," he said. "Mrs. Morgan is here, and

Mrs. Conners, not to mention the children."

"They cannot take the place of a husband, although they have perhaps been expected to of late," she said. "If you are going to be out, and he is to be here, then I will plan to be out as well."

He gave her a hard look and she half-expected him to forbid her going out alone; instead, he said, "That will not be necessary. Al Zaghral will be with me for the evening. It is an important deal. I will need his help in negotiating it."

She concealed the sense of triumph this gave her, and only said, "Thank you." She did not apologize for her feelings toward the man; it could not be a secret that she detested him, and she would not play the hypocrite in that regard, even though she did find it necessary to deceive her husband.

But she had been fooled before when, thinking Al Zaghral was away, she had gone to that room, only to confront him again. This time she was determined to make sure of his whereabouts, and when she thought the time was right for them to be engaged at the club, she asked Mrs. Conners to send Glade to her.

"I want you to go to my husband's club,"

she told him; she had sent him there a few times before with messages for Joseph.

"Yes, ma'am," he said with his usual sober air. "Shall I be carrying a message?"

"No," she said. "I only want to know if he is there."

"Shall I tell him —"

"Tell him nothing," she answered sharply. "You are not to speak to him at all, nor ask to see him. You are only to inquire at the door if he is there." She paused and added, "And you are to ask if he is accompanied by his assistant. Do you understand?"

"Yes, ma'am," Glade said, nodding his head. "You want to know if they are there, and then I'm to come back and let you know."

"Exactly," she said. She smiled and patted his shoulder in conspiratorial fashion, although she was sure he had no idea the importance of his mission.

In fact, Glade had rightly guessed that her interest was in the whereabouts of Al Zaghral and not of her husband. The boy was also frightened of the Oriental, although the man had hardly said a dozen words to him since he had come into the house. Glade sensed that there was a contest of wills raging in the house. He knew

149

nothing of its nature, but his sympathies were entirely with the beautiful young woman who had befriended him and his family. Had Liza asked him, he would have refused her nothing, not even murder.

Now, instinctively understanding that she wanted his inquiry to be as secret as possible, he went beyond her instructions. He did not inquire at the door of the club at all. He had previously observed that a large elm tree grew conveniently near the windows of the club. It was the sort of tree that constituted an invitation to a boy, and it was a simple enough matter for him to make his own inquiries by climbing the tree and looking inside.

He was able to return quickly to tell his mistress that her husband was indeed at his club, at dinner, with Al Zaghral and some other men whom he did not know.

"Did they learn you were asking after them?" she asked, nervousness making her voice a trifle unsteady.

"No, ma'am," he assured her confidently.

This was the opportunity she had been waiting for; when she had sent Glade back to his own room, she went to the desk and brought out the hammer she had already placed there. Steeling herself, she once again mounted the stairs toward the room in which the gem waited.

The house lay silent about her, its very emptiness seeming to echo with warnings. The rooms of the servants were far enough away that they would not hear what she was doing; even had they done so she felt sure they would not interfere.

She came into the room. It was dim, with only that faint, eerie glow from the pedestal. This time she did not mean to waste time looking for a way to remove the glass case. She came up to the pedestal and lifted the hammer to strike.

A hand came down upon her shoulder. She gave a cry and turned to find herself once again facing Al Zaghral. This time his smile was an unconcealed sneer.

"You little fool," he said, his voice a sibilant whisper. "You are as foolish as you are lovely. Haven't you realized yet that you cannot have the ruby unless I give it to you? It is mine, just as your husband is mine. Just as you too will be mine."

He drew her toward him. In horror she realized that he meant to embrace her, to kiss her. In her hand she still held the hammer and she swung out savagely with it at his face. She did not care if she hurt him, she wanted to smash that sneer from his face. At that moment she was capable of anything, even murder.

He struck the hammer from her hand as easily as if he were swatting away a fly. He seized her wrist in his fingers, his grip like iron, and pulled her roughly against him. He lowered his face toward hers. She tried to scream, but her scream was smothered as his mouth came down upon hers, his evil, sensual mouth with its rotted teeth and its foul breath.

She was sick with disgust and revulsion. His embrace was like an iron band holding her against him. She could not move, she could not escape him. Her head swam. Only the fear of what more he would do if she fainted allowed her to cling to her consciousness.

At last his lips left hers. Nausea threatened, but her voice was even as she spoke.

"Let me go," she said. Her words dripped with the hatred she felt for him.

Almost to her surprise he did as she said, releasing her so suddenly that she nearly fell. Her legs felt unsteady and rubbery, as if they would not support her. Her cheeks burned crimson, and to her further shame she began to cry.

"It is no use," he said. "You will be mine,

I swear it. In time you will come to me and ask me to take you."

She could not trust her voice to speak. She turned and ran from him. This time his laugh was loud, a laugh of triumph, echoing along the halls after her as she ran.

Chapter 13

Her tears burned like hot streams across her cheeks. In her room she pushed a chair against the door. She went to her closet and dragged out the portmanteau that was pushed back into the corner. She began haphazardly to drag clothes from their hangers and cram them into the case, hardly caring how they were packed. All she could think of was that she must flee. She could no longer stay in the same house with that monster, now knowing that he desired her. There was no safety here for her, no protection. Joseph was his servant, there was no one to help her but her housekeeper or her maid and two small children.

She fastened her bag and, half-carrying, half-dragging it, she came to the door. She listened, but there was no sound from without. Holding her breath she opened the door a crack and looked out.

No one. The hall was empty. Tugging her portmanteau along the corridor, she made her way clumsily down the stairs.

Below, she pulled the bellrope to summon Mrs. Conners.

"Have the carriage brought around," she ordered when Mrs. Conners appeared.

She had not bothered to wash her face and knew that it was tear-streaked. She had thrust a hat on her head without regard for appearance, and it sat askew, half over one side of her forehead. She looked beside herself with frenzy.

"Is anything wrong?" Mrs. Conners asked, concern overriding her awareness of her station.

"No, no, just call the carriage, please," Liza cried.

But when Mrs. Conners had gone to do her bidding, Liza sank into a divan and buried her face in her hands. Her flight had lost its original impetus, her hysteria had begun to spend itself.

How could she leave? How could she abandon her husband, knowing that his life, his very soul might be at stake? Flee because she had been frightened like a rabbit? Where was the courage with which she had vowed to fight that wicked man? Where was the love she had sworn for Joseph? Love would not turn tail and run at the first fright, surely.

She gave a despairing sigh and raised her

chin, brushing her hair back from her face. When Mrs. Conners returned to tell her that the carriage was ready, she found her mistress standing in the parlor, disconsolate but calm.

"It's all right," Liza told her. "I won't need the carriage now. I am not leaving."

When she was calmer and had returned her things to her room, Liza made her way down to the library. This was much unchanged from the way it had been when Clark Rutherford lived here. He had been a prodigious reader as well as a traveler — and she had had a new idea. Uncle Clark had known of the ruby's existence before he had obtained it on his last journey. Perhaps he had read of it in one of his books; if so, that book might offer her some clue to the mystery of the stone.

She stood in the center of the room and gazed around her at the hundreds of volumes lining the walls. She had no idea where to begin; the task suddenly looked awesome.

A sudden noise nearby frightened her. Her heart pounded as she turned, expecting to see her tormentor by her again. Instead, she saw young Glade, about to steal from the room.

"Glade," she said, surprised and relieved at the same time.

"I'm sorry," he said, coming to a halt. "I didn't think anyone came in here at this time. I was just doing a little reading."

"Why, that's perfectly all right," she said. "I told you to make use of the books here. But wait," she added in a more hopeful tone. "Have you really looked over many of these books?"

"Some," he said, nodding.

She tried not to be too optimistic; it was doubtful really that a boy would have paid any attention to the sort of books she was looking for.

"Tell me," she said, "have you by any chance run across any books on . . . well, let me see . . . on rubies, for instance?"

He was thoughtful for a moment. Then, wordlessly, he went to the cabinet and removed an old leather-bound volume which he brought to her.

She examined it; it was a book on precious gems. She flipped through its pages but saw nothing that looked promising. Perhaps after all her idea had not been such a good one.

Glade meanwhile had returned to the shelves and was peering at the titles along one shelf. He pulled out a book and brought this one to her also.

Stones of Legend was the title.

"This looks more like it," she said, her spirits picking up again. She riffled its pages and at once saw Uncle Clark's handwriting in the margins. Her pulse quickened.

"Do you want any more?" Glade asked.

"No — wait," she said. "Let me look at this. Stay, please, go on with your reading. I'll let you know what else I need."

He seemed content to return to the big leather chair in which he had been reading before. He returned his attention to his book, only occasionally glancing toward his mistress to see if she had any need of his services.

She had gone to a chair by a window and was lost in the book Glade had brought her. The book fell open in her hands to a page on which Clark had made several notations. With mounting interest she saw that it was the section on rubies. The "Lord of Gems," the author called the stone, noting that it was the birthstone for July.

"The ruby is still the rarest of all stones," she read. "It has always possessed an other-world quality. In the ancient legends of the Orient the ruby is said to contain the original spark of life, 'a deep drop of the heart's blood of Mother Earth.' Of great rarity and matchless beauty, the ruby is prized by many above the diamond. Its name comes from *ruber*, the Latin word for red. During the Middle Ages this name was used for all red stones, so that the word ruby has been falsely applied to all red gems of the period."

She read quickly over the dry background information — that ruby was a form of the mineral corundum, that its color derives from chromium, that it was the second hardest of all gems, after the diamond.

"Star rubies are gems containing a double refraction of light, brought out in the cutting process; the result is an apparent star of radiant white light caught and imbedded in the stone.

"The finest and rarest rubies are called pigeon's blood, or blood rubies," she read. Uncle Clark had underlined the latter phrase. She remembered his describing his stone as a blood ruby.

"The blood rubies are found only in Mogok, Burma; these mines have been in operation for centuries.

"Since flawless rubies are rare they are highly prized and expensive. There have been attempts to imitate rubies, but thus far success has been limited. Because of their rarity, the number of famous stones is less than one might otherwise expect. The writers of the ancient Orient tell of dazzling stones, and certain rajahs and potentates have possessed striking examples.

"The oldest account of a ruby was made by Marco Polo. He wrote of a ruby he saw that was owned by the King of Ceylon: 'It is a span long, as thick as a man's arm, and without a flaw.' The thirteenth century Emperor of China, the Kublai Khan, offered the value of a city for it, and was told by the Ceylonese King that he would not part with it 'if all the treasures of the world were laid at his feet.'

"The Black Prince's Ruby was given to the King of England in 1367 by the King of Castile.

"The largest ruby known is the Timur Ruby, which belonged to many rulers of India and Persia, for their names are carved in Arabic on the reverse side. It dates back to 1398. At one time it was the property of Shah Jahan, who built the Taj Mahal.

"In antiquity the ruby was the symbol of friendship. In India the stones were thought to possess caste, the deeper colors

160

being of the highest caste; the paler the color, the lower the caste. If a stone of the highest caste came into contact with one of a lower caste, supernatural powers were said to be attached to them.

"The ancient Orientals regarded the ruby as self-luminous. It was called the 'glowing stone' or 'lamp stone,' and one Chinese Emperor had in his chamber in one of the pillars of gold a 'ruby half-a-foot in length, that in the night seemeth so large and clear and shining that it is as light as day.' "

Liza thought of the eerie glow possessed by the ruby in the room above. Had it only been a trick of her imagination, or did it in fact possess a mystical light of its own?

She was about to conclude that her search was fruitless when she turned a page and came to a section heavily underlined in Uncle Clark's pen:

"Perhaps the most famous, or infamous, of all gems is the so-called Baghdad Ruby. Neither the exact source of this stone nor its present whereabouts is known, but legends concerning it and its powers date throughout the centuries. One King of Siam attributed his amazing appearance of youth, even when he neared one hundred, to the magic of the stone. Others have named it the source of great wealth and power.

"But the stone is cursed. It is said to be the property of Eblis, who demands the soul of the stone's owner in return for the wealth and power he gives them. The soul in turn becomes one of the wicked jinn serving Eblis."

There the chapter of rubies ended. Liza closed the book thoughtfully.

Eblis, she thought. Uncle Clark had mentioned him too, but she could not recall exactly what he had said.

"Glade," she said, rousing the boy again from the book in which he had become absorbed. "Do you think you could find me a book on mythology, the mythology of . . ." she hesitated. "Well, of the East."

He went to do her bidding, and in a few minutes returned. To her dismay this time he brought an entire stack of books. She groaned inwardly and took them from him, thanking him. She returned to her chair and began to leaf through them.

It was in the third book that she found a paragraph on Eblis:

"In Muslim legend, Eblis is the Devil, called Azazel before the fall; he rules over the evil genii or jinn. When Adam was created, Allah commanded all the angels to worship him, but Azazel replied, 'Me thou hast created of smokeless fire, and shall I reverence a creature made of dust?' Allah was angry at this insolent answer and turned the disobedient angel into a Sheytan, or devil, and Azazel became Eblis, the father of devils."

Liza closed the book. Eblis, the father of devils — and the true master of the Baghdad ruby. And, unless she could somehow prevent it, master of Joseph's soul as well.

Chapter 14

The discovery of the identity of her antagonist was almost enough to send Liza again into flight. Before she had feared and hated him, but now the very thought of him filled her with dread. She went to any lengths to avoid coming into contact with him. The sound of his footsteps in the hall would send her cowering into a room, hiding behind a door until he was past.

As for Joseph, while it was not possible that he could live in the same house and remain unaware of her terror, he gave no indication that he took the slightest notice of it. Indeed, during the period he took little enough notice of her. Christmas was drawing nearer and it should have been a lovely season; in the past, when they had been poor, they had always greatly enjoyed the holiday season together. This year she felt anything but joyful, and so far as she could see Joseph remained unaware of the season altogether.

That was why she was so surprised when he suggested in an entirely offhand manner, that they have a party.

"We've always had some sort of get-together for the holidays," he said. "This year for a change we'll be able to afford it."

"You speak as if we lived in abject poverty in the past," she said.

"Looking back, it almost seems as if we did," he said.

"There are different kinds of poverty," she said. "There is a poverty of the spirit that is far worse than a mere lack of money."

He was silent for a moment. For once he regarded her with something other than indifference; he seemed actually to be contemplating what she had said, and for a brief instant she thought she saw in his eyes a flicker of sadness.

"Whatever I have done," he said in a low voice, "I have done for you. It was for you that I desired wealth, power, magnificence."

His words fanned the fire of hope that had burned low within her. She ran to him and threw herself into his arms.

"Oh, my darling," she said. "If that is so, then do one thing more for me, dispose of it. I never wanted it, nor have I enjoyed it. Rid us of it, and of its hateful source."

She felt him stiffen in her arms and

knew that she had struck a raw nerve.

"You mean the ruby," he said.

"Joseph, Joseph!" she cried, clinging to him. "Can't you see? It's evil, it's destroying you. That man is —"

He thrust her away from him suddenly. "We'll talk no more about this," he said firmly. His jaw was set in a stubborn line.

"But we must," she said. "We must."

"I forbid it," he said, his voice rising. "I've taken a vow, I made a bargain. There is no turning back now, and I warn you, it is you who will destroy us both with your meddling. I forbid you to discuss this again, and I forbid you to continue your childish efforts to dispose of the ruby."

With that he strode from the room, leaving her in futile tears.

He had not, however, withdrawn his suggestion that they have a party, and she seized upon that with an almost frenzied enthusiasm. Perhaps to have their friends around them again, to give Joseph a glimpse of their former life . . . maybe even one of their friends would speak to him, say something to him that would restore his sense of balance. Anything was better than to continue their tortured isolation in this house.

Despite the short notice, nearly everyone

accepted the invitations she sent out. She had no doubt that some of them were merely curious; this was the first they had entertained since coming into wealth and moving to Sea Cliff.

As the date drew nearer, her excitement mounted — to see friends again, to laugh and be merry, to forget the nightmare that surrounded her there. She worked tirelessly at the preparations, fairly exhausting Mrs. Conners and Mrs. Morgan. But she was careful of the money she spent; she did not want to be indebted to that wicked creature. She would not sully her soul with the wealth his evil bargain had produced.

It was the day of the party, early in the afternoon, and she was hanging the last of the Christmas decorations when she had an unexpected caller. She heard the doorbell, and heard Mrs. Morgan's heavy tread as she went to answer it. After a moment, Mrs. Morgan appeared in the doorway.

"Begging your pardon, ma'am," she said, with a strangely embarrassed air, "but you've got a caller, a gentleman."

Liza, atop a small ladder to hang a garland, said, "A stranger, you mean?"

"No, ma'am, he's not exactly a stranger." Mrs. Morgan hesitated. "It's Mr. Whitney, ma'am."

"Bill?" Liza dropped the garland from her hands. "Bill Whitney?" She gave a little cry of delight and jumped down from her perch, running for the hall.

"Bill!" she cried. "What a pleasant surprise!"

In the hall she stopped. Had she not been forewarned, she might not even have recognized the man standing just inside the door. His hair was long and uncombed, and he had not shaved in several days. It was longer than that since his clothes, if clothes they could be called, had been washed. They were filthy rags that promised but scant protection from the winter winds.

"Hello, Liza," he said, remaining where he was. "Surprised to see me?"

"Oh, Bill, what's happened?" she said, unable to conceal her dismay. She saw before her, superimposed as it were over the actual man, an image of the way he had looked before, so neat, so correct, full of life and vitality.

"Funny you should ask that question," he said, coming nearer. "Could I have a drink, Liza?"

"Of course," she said quickly, leading him into the parlor. "Brandy?"

"Please." He looked around, taking in

the party preparations, the gay decorations. "You look splendid, I must say."

"Thank you," she said, bringing him the drink.

He sipped at it and regarded her over its rim. "You can't very well say the same for me, can you?"

She sighed and moved to a chair. "I can't pretend to understand," she said. "When you left the company, Joseph said he had provided for you most generously. I even went to your boarding house, but you'd already moved out."

"Did you now?" he asked, smiling. "That's nice to hear. I thought no one cared what happened to me."

"But that's nonsense, you know I do. And Joseph does too, if you only knew it. You judge him too harshly."

"Do I?" He laughed sardonically. "It was Joseph who fired me. He threw me out into the street with no notice, no pay, without a single thought for how or whether I would survive."

"But he said —"

"He lied," Bill interrupted her curtly.

She stared at him in dismay. She thought back to the day he had been fired; Joseph had been angry, he might have acted impetuously — but he had told her otherwise.

Yet she knew, as she stared at Bill, that it was Joseph who had lied. The evidence was there before her, in Bill's destitute condition.

Pity moved her to stand and go to him, taking his hand in her own. "Bill, I can't tell you how sorry I am," she said.

He put his drink aside and clasped both of her hands. "It is almost worth everything I've gone through to hear you say that," he said.

"If there is anything I can do to make it up to you, I hope you will tell me what it is. I have an allowance for running the house, let me give you what I have."

"It isn't money I want from you," he said in a husky voice.

She raised her eyes to his and saw the old familiar look, the look of desire that had so annoyed her before.

"Bill, I —" she said, but he cut her words off.

"Liza, darling, you know I love you," he said. "I've always loved you."

He tried to kiss her. She turned her lips aside and his kiss landed on her cheek. For a moment he held her to him. The suddenly, angrily, he released her and turned away.

"If I had that ruby of your husband's you

wouldn't turn away from me like that," he said in a petulant voice.

"Don't say that," she said. "You don't know."

"I know that it's given him everything in the world he wants, money, wealth, power. I tell you I'd gladly sell my soul, if that's the price, to get my hands on that stone."

His words seemed to reverberate in her mind. She thought of her futile efforts to get rid of the stone, of her prayers for help in freeing her husband from its curse — and now here before her was a man willing to go to any lengths to obtain possession of the stone.

"What would you do to get the stone?" she asked slowly.

He turned to face her again. When he saw that she was serious the anger began to fade from his face, to be replaced by something that she liked even less.

"I told you," he said. "I'd do anything."

"What if you had the opportunity to . . . ," she paused, "to steal it?"

"Is it here?" he asked quickly, his eyes darting about the room as if he expected to see the stone on display.

"It is in the house," she said. "Only there is someone who guards it carefully."

"Al Zaghral?"

She nodded. "He seems to be never far from the ruby."

"There must be some time . . . Liza, will you help me?"

For a long moment they exchanged searching looks. Finally she said, "We are having some people in tonight for a party. If you were to come, I would tell Joseph that I just ran into you and invited you. He can hardly throw you out."

"I don't know, he might."

"He won't, I'll see to that," she promised. "And I will see that Al Zaghral is occupied while you go for the ruby. The rest is up to you."

"Why are you willing to do this?" he asked. "I know that you don't love me."

"No, I love my husband," she said. "That is why."

Chapter 15

The party had been completely eclipsed in her thoughts, and when at last she began to dress for it, it was with a kind of dread fascination.

She had chosen a white gown, trimmed in ermine; but when she had donned it and looked at herself in the mirror, she found herself irritated by its pristine look. She rummaged impatiently through the dresses in her closet, many of them as yet unworn, and settled at last upon a dark-green velvet trimmed in brown. She was still not pleased with her appearance; her face had lost all its color and the rouge she applied only gave her an artificial doll-like aspect.

The guests had already begun to arrive by the time she descended the great staircase. Mrs. Conners, crisp and starched-looking, was at the door, and Liza saw her husband chatting amiably with a group of new arrivals. For a moment she paused, staring down at him. He looked so handsome and, from here, so unchanged. She found herself wondering if she had only been having some sort of nightmare — how could it be real, any of it? How could her beloved Joseph be in league with the devil himself? How could a gem, a ruby, however precious, grant a man's wishes, and simultaneously doom him?

She nearly laughed at herself, at all her fears and anxieties. But just then another figure separated himself from a cluster of men and moved to Joseph's side.

Al Zaghral. She saw him lean close and whisper something, and Joseph nodded. The two of them moved off together.

She steeled herself, pulling her shoulders back bravely, and went on down the stairs, holding her long full skirt up slightly.

Helen Cook saw her and hurried to meet her at the bottom of the stairs. They had been schoolmates together and the closest of friends for as long as Liza could recall. With a shock she realized now that she had not seen Helen in months, not since Joseph had come into possession of the ruby and changed their lives.

"Liza, how wonderful to see you again," Helen cried, flinging her arms about her friend. "I thought perhaps you spent all your time these days in the cellar counting your money."

"Not my money," Liza said, returning

the embrace. "Happy holiday, Helen, you look wonderful."

Helen, who had put on weight to the point of plumpness, did nevertheless look wonderful; she exuded an air of radiant good health and good cheer that camouflaged any flaws in her appearance.

She was also outspoken. She drew back from Liza and studied her with a frankly critical eye. "I wish I could say the same for you," she said.

Liza laughed nervously. "Have I aged so badly in the months since I last saw you?"

"Yes," Helen said bluntly. "What is it? Joseph beating you with a cane, or what?"

"Joseph wouldn't hurt a flea, you know that," Liza said.

"I used to know that, but lately I hear different things about him. Of course I was quick to discount all of them, until this minute, when I saw how haggard you look. Honestly, you look as if you hadn't had a good night's sleep in months, your color is off, I don't . . ."

She left her remark unfinished as others, having caught sight of Liza, began to drift over to greet her. Liza glued a smile to her face and greeted each of them in turn, chatting about the holiday and the weather, and Joseph's remarkable good fortune these days.

Yet while she talked brightly and smiled at those around her, her thoughts were on Helen's remarks.

So, she thought, people were already talking about Joseph. His reputation before had been spotless; she could not but wonder how badly he had damaged it in the past few months.

She was less concerned about how badly she looked, except that that too must reflect on Joseph, as it had in Helen's mind. Other than that, what did she care about her looks? Before, her beauty had been a gift that she had brought to the man she loved, holding it as a casket of jewels in her hands, and offering it humbly to him. But now the jewels seemed false, the casket valueless.

"For Heaven's sake," Helen whispered to her in a pause, "stop smiling like that."

"Like what?"

"Like a stone griffin."

Mrs. Conners was admitting another guest. Liza's heart skipped a beat when she recognized Bill. He had gotten a good suit of clothes from somewhere, probably borrowed, and he had shaved and groomed himself neatly. He looked, if not the Bill

Whitney of old, at least respectable again.

His eyes went to hers immediately as he came into the room, as if this were a scene in a play that they had rehearsed a hundred times over. Liza felt her hand shake and had to put aside the glass of sherry she was drinking.

She looked around quickly and saw Joseph. In the same instant, he saw Bill. She saw his smile fade, his jaw tense. He excused himself and began to make his way toward the doorway where Bill was still standing.

"Excuse me," Liza said, interrupting a grey-bearded man in the middle of some sentence, the sense of which had completely eluded her. She hurried past him, intercepting her husband in mid-room.

"I invited him," she said softly, putting her hand on his arm.

He looked coldly down at her, but the coldness was all in his eyes. No one watching them would have suspected the angry tension crackling between them, nor the fear in her heart.

"When did you do that?" he asked.

"This afternoon. I was out shopping, and I passed him on the street. It was such a surprise, and I thought of the party. It seemed the friendly thing to do. We haven't seen Bill in so long."

She was talking quickly, partly because she was nervous and partly because she had rehearsed in her mind what she would say, and she wanted to get it all said before he cut her off. She had planned all day to say something to Joseph, but she had not been able to screw up her courage, and finally it had been too late; she had decided to wait until Bill appeared. After all, he might have lost his nerve, too.

But now here he was, and Joseph looked entirely displeased with her.

"It was a damned foolish thing to do," he said in a low voice. His glance went to Bill, who still had not moved into the room. "I can't think why he was fool enough to come here."

"Perhaps he merely wanted to see us," she said. She knew that Joseph had lost the resolution that had propelled him in Bill's direction, the decision to evict him from the party. She did not wait for him to change his mind again.

"Let us at least be polite to him," she said, patting his arm. "It would spoil the party otherwise."

She left him and hurried to Bill. She knew that several people had observed the little scene being played, and she was careful to keep her greeting friendly but no more than that.

"Bill, how good to see you," she said, letting him take her hand briefly in his.

"I can't tell you how excited I am to be here," he said, and his smile was faintly mocking.

She waited until the party was at its peak before again seeking Bill's company. Having greeted him, she had let him drift into the crowd of people in the room, and had forced herself to play the role of hostess. As the time passed, she had known that she must soon send Bill for the ruby; certainly she was aware of the importance, to her and Joseph especially, of the success of their efforts; yet she continued to put off the fateful moment.

At last, however, it could be put off no longer if it were to happen at all. She saw Bill watching her steadily from across the room, and knew that the time had come. Slowly, still postponing the event, she moved across the room to him.

"It's getting late," he said when they had moved safely off to an unoccupied corner of the room.

"Yes, I know," she said. She hesitated for a moment. When she began to speak, she spoke all in a rush, her words running together so that he had to listen very carefully.

"You'll have to go up the back stairs," she said, "The main ones are too conspicuous. Through the kitchen. Tell Mrs. Morgan you're running an errand for me if she asks. Through the washroom, the narrow door on the left. On the third floor, the second door along the hall on the right."

"Is it locked?"

She shook her head. "It never is. The stone is under glass. I don't know how to open the case."

"I'll open it," he said confidently. "And you will be?"

"With him," she said, not needing to identify him further.

He moved as if to go but she put out her hand. "Wait. Give me a few minutes. Wait until you see that I have him occupied before you slip out."

He nodded and she left him, moving as if without purpose about the room. She saw Al Zaghral, standing quite by himself, watching the party's progress with a faint smile of amusement. She shuddered as she looked at him, remembering the moment upstairs when he had seized her and kissed her.

He saw her, his gaze fastening itself on her. She moved toward him.

"May I speak with you?" she asked.

He looked more amused than surprised. "But of course," he said. "Need it be private?"

"I think it should be. May we go in here?" She indicated a door near where he was standing, which led to a small sitting room, rarely used.

He gestured with his hand for her to lead the way. She went with heavy steps toward the door. The thought of being alone in the room with him filled her with dread, but it must be done.

She put her hand to the door and as she did so glanced over her shoulder. At the same moment she saw Bill slip unnoticed through the door to the kitchen.

"Is something wrong?"

She started at the sound of Al Zaghral's voice, so near her ear. She had been unaware that she was standing frozen. An observer would have thought she was listening for some foreign sound.

In fact, she had been struck by a vision of Bill, in the room above, taking the ruby into his hand. Suddenly she thought of what she was doing. She was condemning him, she saw that now, condemning him to a fate the full horrors of which he could not possibly realize. She might as well put a gun to his head and pull the trigger; that would be kinder, surely.

And as quickly she knew that she could not go through with their scheme. This was what had troubled her throughout the evening, this was why she had put off and put off the moment of decision.

She looked once at Al Zaghral. The way he watched her frightened her, as if he could read her thoughts.

"Please," she said, putting her hand to her temple. "Excuse me, I'll be back in a moment."

She did not wait for his reply but hurried away from the room. She went directly up the main stairs, holding her skirt high to allow her to run. A sense of urgency drove her, so that she hardly cared what anyone thought who saw her; she felt that she must reach Bill before he reached the ruby, before he actually took it in his hands. She must somehow dissuade him from that course.

She met him in the hall, just outside the room. He looked rightly startled to see her.

"What's happened?" he asked in a whisper.

She was out of breath and for a moment

she could only stand silently before him, her breasts rising and falling with the effort of her breathing.

He took her shoulders and drew her into the shadow of a doorway. "Has something gone wrong?" he demanded tensely.

"No, only, I can't let you do it!"

He looked first surprised, then angry. "In the name of God, why not?" he asked.

"I . . . I don't think I can explain, really," she said.

"You'll damned well have to if you expect to talk me out of this."

"The curse, the curse on the ruby, it's real. Bill, I know it sounds crazy, but there is really a curse on it. Al Zaghral —"

"You little fool," he said, shaking her. "Do you think I care about a curse? Do you think I care about anything so long as I get that stone? I told you, I'd do anything, even sell my soul. If that's what that devil Al Zaghral wants, he's welcome to it, it's no good to me, anyway. But first I mean to have the stone in my possession. Possession is nine-tenths of the law, as they say."

"Bill —"

"No, listen to me," he said firmly. "You go back down there and see that he's occupied, and leave the ruby and the curse to me. You want to save your husband, don't you?"

"Yes," she said weakly.

"Do you think I didn't know that's why you're helping me? But I don't care, so long as you do help me. And you will, won't you, if not for your sake, for Joseph's?"

For a long moment she stared into his eyes. Finally she nodded. "Heaven help me, yes, I will," she said.

He watched her move away, retracing her steps to the party. He thought how much he had once loved her, how his body had ached with desire for her.

That was in the past now. He had only one desire to obtain the ruby and its power. What did physical lust matter in comparison to that? And love — what had it been for him but an agony? He had been a fool all his life. He had prayed and prayed that somehow the woman he loved would be his, and his prayers had been ignored. Very well, if God would not negotiate with him, then the devil would.

She disappeared down the stairs. He turned from the empty hall and reached his hand out for the doorknob behind him. He held his breath, half-expecting some disappointment.

It was unlocked. The knob turned, the door opened. He stepped into the room, and stopped. There before him was the pedestal, with its glass case, and there in the case was the ruby, glowing eerily.

He took a step forward — and heard an echoing step behind him.

Chapter 16

At first, as she descended the long staircase, she could not think what it was that was bothering her, some realization at the back of her mind like a name you cannot quite recall. It was not until she reached the last landing that she realized consciously what it was.

Quiet. The normal sounds of a large gathering of people had dwindled down to a faint murmur. As she came in sight of the main corridor she saw why. People were leaving.

Joseph was in the hall saying good-night to a small cluster of their guests. The front parlor was all but empty. At the door people were struggling into their wraps.

"What's going on?" she asked of her husband, coming up to him. He had separated himself from their departing guests when he saw her and started toward her.

"Our guests are going home," he said.

"So I can see, but why? It's so early, I don't understand."

"As to why, I asked them to leave. I ex-

186

plained that you had retired to your room because you were not feeling well."

She stared in astonishment at him. For a moment she could think of nothing to say. She shook her head as if she might thus clear her mind of the entire scene.

"Liza, dear, good-night," Helen said, hurrying over. "I hope you're feeling better soon. I'd love to get together for a chat."

Helen looked so plainly worried that for her sake Liza smiled bravely. "Yes, let's do that," she said. "Have a nice Christmas."

In another few minutes they were gone. The door closed after the last of them and Liza found herself alone in the hall with her husband.

"I hope you will explain," she said coldly.

He shrugged and said, "I thought it time the party ended. You had left, I assumed you thought the same."

"What outrageous nonsense," she said, too angry to care if they quarrelled. "I was with Al Zaghral, I told him that I would be back in —"

She stopped, remembering. She suddenly left her husband and hurried to the doorway to the front parlor. It was empty but for the debris left behind.

"Where is he?" She demanded, turning back to her husband.

"I'm not sure I know who you mean," her husband said.

Her eyes were wide with fright. She thought of Bill in the room above, thinking himself safe from detection. She thought of Al Zaghral; she thought there were no limits to what he might be capable of.

She ran to the stairs, flinging herself up them with all the speed she could muster. She did not even look back to see if Joseph followed her or not.

She reached the second floor, then the third. As she started down that long corridor she saw Mrs. Morgan emerge from the door that opened onto the back stairs.

She had hardly taken three steps along the hall when she heard a shriek. It was a scream of agony, that ended as abruptly as if cut off by a knife. Both she and Mrs. Morgan froze in their tracks, staring along the long distance of the hall at one another.

Liza gave a little cry as a hand came down on her shoulder. It was Joseph. So, he had followed her after all. Perhaps he knew what had happened.

"Mrs. Morgan," he said, "I would appreciate it if you forgot you heard that sound."

It was said quietly, pleasantly enough, and yet there was an underlying air of menace that made it authoritative, that made it a command, and warned not to disobey.

Mrs. Morgan looked at her and at him. She did not so much as glance toward the room from which the scream had come. After a moment, without a word, she turned and disappeared again down the back stairs.

They found Bill's body two days later at the bottom of the cliff. It had been pounded by the waves against the rocks, so that, as she understood it, he was hardly recognizable as a human corpse, let alone as Bill Whitney, but his identification was unscathed.

By that time, Mrs. Morgan had gone. She came to Liza the morning after the party, to announce her decision.

"Ma'am, I feel that I've got to give my notice," she said, standing with her arms folded sternly across her bosom.

Liza, who was embroidering her husband's initials on a set of handkerchiefs for him, paused in her work and looked sadly up at the housekeeper.

"Yes, I can see that you would feel that way," she said. "How soon will you be leaving?"

"Right away," Mrs. Morgan said quickly, adding in a voice that pleaded for understanding, "It's best that I do, ma'am. If anyone was to come and talk to me about . . . about the other evening, you see I couldn't lie and say I didn't hear anything, the way your husband wants me to do. I'd have to tell what I heard, you see. And anyway, you've got Mrs. Conners, she won't be leaving you, and she's fit to take over as housekeeper."

"Yes, of course." There was an awkward little silence. "We shall miss you, I'm sure you know that."

"And I'll miss you, ma'am, well you know," Mrs. Morgan said. "You know it breaks my heart to go, but there's things a person oughtn't to have to put up with, as I see it, and there's things that just aren't right around here. I don't know exactly what is going on these days, but it ain't what it used to be, and it ain't right, I know that much. I don't know as you know yourself what's happening, ma'am, but it's the Gospel truth, you ought to leave with me, and the Lord forgive me for saying it."

"But I could hardly do that," Liza said calmly, "as my husband is here. My place is with him."

"Yes, ma'am," Mrs. Morgan said, looking

rebuffed. "And my place is out of here. Merry Christmas, and God bless you."

"God bless you, too, and Merry Christmas," Liza said sadly.

When the police came to question them about Bill's death, Mrs. Morgan was already gone, and there was no reason for them to think of questioning her. Mrs. Conners had heard and seen nothing, she had been too busy with the party. Liza sat and listened to the Inspector question Joseph. She saw, and saw that the Inspector must have seen, too, that Joseph was nervous and ill-at-ease. Perhaps, she thought, nothing before had come quite so close to him as this. It gave her an odd sense of hope, for it revealed to her that he was not yet completely lost to decency, that she might yet be able to free him from the curse of the ruby, and have him back as the good, honorable man he had been before. If only . . .

"You have nothing to add to what your husband has told us, Mrs. Hanson?"

She realized that they were all looking at her and that her thoughts had drifted away. She was surprised at how calm she felt.

"Nothing," she said.

"You were busy with your guests?"

"Yes, and then I had a headache, so I

went up to my room for a short while."

"You do not know exactly when Mr. Whitney left the party?" The Inspector was watching her closely; it unnerved her a little, but still she managed to answer in an even voice.

"No. He was gone when I came down."

"And you have no idea why he might have gone out to the cliff?"

"Perhaps," she said, "he wanted a breath of air. It was close in here, so many people, you understand. Of course, that is only conjecture."

Unexpectedly, Inspector Berthold said, "Mr. Whitney was in love with you, was he not?"

"I object to that question," Joseph said sharply, standing.

Liza could feel her cheeks turning crimson, but she managed to answer, "I believe people thought so."

"Did he never declare his feelings?"

"He . . ." She hesitated, then went on. "He told me once that he loved me." She avoided looking at her husband.

"Recently?"

"Yes." She found herself looking down at her hands. She had been wringing them together. She stopped, and held them flat in her lap.

"Did your husband know of this?"

Joseph said, "I have long been aware that Mr. Whitney was infatuated with my wife. It was not an unusual situation. She is, you no doubt have seen for yourself, an extremely lovely woman. I have no doubt that many men have seen her and fancied themselves in love with her. If you are suggesting, however, that anything improper might have occurred between my wife and Mr. Whitney —"

"I would not dream of such a suggestion," Berthold interjected.

"— I will have to ask you to leave my house. Nor, might I add, did I murder Mr. Whitney in a fit of jealous passion. Of my wife's propriety and fidelity I am utterly confident. It is not in me to be jealous of a foolish young man's dreams."

Inspector Berthold rose, too, folding his notebook closed. "Alas," he said, "this foolish young man's dreams are ended."

On that sobering note, he left.

She saw the policeman again when she went to Bill's funeral. She had not asked Joseph if she might go, nor did he offer to accompany her. She went alone, standing in the falling snow at the gravesite while the minister hurried through his final remarks. In the distance the church bells chimed a Christmas carol; the notes rolled across the cemetery, seeming to hover in confusion amid the homes of the dead, then vanished on the winter wind.

She cried at the end, not for the lifeless thing in the coffin, but for the man who had been. She thought that, although he had never possessed it, he too had been destroyed by the ruby.

And, she added silently, by greed.

Inspector Berthold followed her at some distance until she had returned to Sea Cliff.

Chapter 17

It was three days before Christmas, then two; finally it was Christmas Eve.

Joseph eyed the calendar with a kind of dread. Somehow as that holy day grew closer he grew more and more unhappy with the situation in which he had become entangled.

It had seemed so simple once, so clear and easy. The promises of wealth, of power; and what did it matter what happened to his soul after he was dead? He had taken the cash and let the credit go.

What he had not realized was that the soul was not given away once in barter, and that was the end of it. It was pared away piece by piece, gain by gain, each day a little of himself torn from him, leaving gaping wounds that ached and bled.

How could he have known that his wife would dread and even hate him? Had he foreseen that he would never have agreed to the infamous bargain, not for any price. Nor had anyone explained that it would cost, not only his soul, but the lives and souls of others. He had not realized that the wealth he would acquire would be minted from the broken lives and hopes of others, like bones ground into meal to feed the evil demon growing within him.

And murder? When had he agreed to murder? His aunt, old, obstinate, stupid even — but he had not wanted her murdered. Dead perhaps, but not murdered. Nor Bill Whitney — a nuisance, of course, and the more so because he was intelligent; but hadn't it been enough to ruin his life?

Tortured by his thoughts, he went out and tried to lose himself in an orgy of shopping. He bought outrageously expensive presents for his wife, knowing even as he bought them that she would not welcome them. That knowledge only drove him to greater extravagance, as if somewhere there was a gift, a price high enough to win her back to him. He did not pause to realize that there was a gift that would accomplish that goal, one still in his power to give, and upon which there was no price.

The tolling of church bells gave him a sudden start. He thought of the Church, of the power of prayer. He had not prayed in years; of late he had not dared.

"If only I could wipe the slate clean," he

thought. He walked slowly to the church and sat down in the rear. At the very least the music would rest his soul, surely.

It was pleasantly dark in the place after the glare of the snowy afternoon. He found it very soothing to listen to the good music. He felt utterly exhausted, and for some minutes he watched the people going to and fro.

He was not far from a confessional. As he watched, a young man, with the look of the country about him, went into the booth. Joseph could hear the faint murmur of words from within. In a few minutes the youth came out and strolled contentedly from the church. He looked so fresh in his simple, rustic clothes; his face glowed with health and innocence. Joseph could hardly restrain a groan of envy. What had that boy to confess? A few foolish mistakes that no doubt brought a smile to the lips of the kind priest, and afterwards his honest spirit was as white as the snow once more.

Suddenly he would have given anything to kneel down and whisper in those gentle ears all that he had gone through; but he knew that he and that priest no longer belonged to the same faith. That priest's soul was God's, while his was bound to the Prince of Darkness.

A procession of seminarists came in. Several of them were quite young. Joseph found himself studying their faces, wondering if any of them had suffered as he was suffering.

The music was good; it had a simple dignity, like the church itself. The service began, but it did not touch him. In his heart he said that it was because God had finally and completely forsaken him. He belonged to Evil and Evil would forever be his companion.

He got up suddenly and half-ran to the door and out into the snowy street. He knew all at once that it was useless to cry and wring his hands, and say that he had not agreed to all the nefarious acts that had been committed in his name, for he had in truth agreed to them. The first time he had turned a deaf ear to another's misery, to another's cry for compassion, he had agreed to all the rest. The first time he had agreed to ruining a man's life, he had committed himself to taking lives. Now the choice was no longer his.

Liza had moved through the days since Bill's death like a sleepwalker. A sense of futility weighed heavily upon her soul. She could think of nothing but the morass into which her husband had sunk, and nightly she prayed for some solution. None came.

Now it was Christmas Eve. The shadows had grown long until at last they had crowded out the day and evening was upon her. Her spirits sank lower with the lowering sun. How could she give thanks for the birth of Jesus when He had abandoned her in her need? How could she celebrate a season of joy when there was only despair in her breast?

She sat down at the piano and attempted to play out her frustrations on the keyboard. She played Chopin, her nimble fingers producing crystalline notes.

She struck a wrong chord and Al Zaghral came into the room.

"Please," he said, coming to stand by the piano, "do not stop playing for my sake."

"My hands are tired," she said, closing the lid on the keyboard.

"You play very well."

She made no reply to this remark. She wanted his compliments no more than she wanted his money. Couldn't he see that she despised him, that she wanted nothing to do with him? Why did he persist in his efforts to be friendly with her, as if they

199

could ever be anything but the bitterest of enemies?

He might have read her thoughts. He said, "You despise me, I suppose."

"Yes," she said. When he made no immediate reply, she asked, "Does that disturb you?"

"Not in the least. But you are a silly little thing, that is all."

"Is it so silly to despise you? I should think it by far the wisest thing to do."

He chuckled softly. "It is nothing to me if you despise me or not. But you are foolish to plot against me, to connive, to bring equally foolish men into the house, all to get what could easily be yours without all that tomfoolery."

At last she raised her eyes and looked at him: she thought he might be teasing her, but he looked entirely serious.

"What do you mean?" she asked.

"The ruby. That is what you want. You have gone to great lengths to obtain it. But you can never do that. No one can. The only way it is possible for anyone to possess it is through my granting it."

The silence of the house seemed to wrap itself about her. She felt as if the temperature had dropped ten, twenty degrees all at once.

"And you would give it to me?"

He shrugged and said, "Perhaps." He went to the table against the wall and poured himself a glass of wine. The light from the chandelier sent slivers of crimson through the liquid in the glass; it reminded her of the glow of the ruby.

"And what is the bargain you are offering me?" she asked.

He smiled. "Perhaps you are not so brave after all. Perhaps it would be more than you are willing to do."

She stood and came to where he stood. "I am not afraid," she said. "You want my soul? Very well then, take it, if you will free my husband from your curse. You must swear that to me."

For a long moment he regarded her steadily. At length he said, "I had something more in mind. Something more than merely your soul."

At first she did not understand. Then, slowly, comprehension came and with it a sense of mounting horror.

"How can you suggest it?" she asked in a whisper. "Knowing how I feel toward you?"

He laughed, revealing his ugly, yellowed teeth. "Love, hate, what is the difference?" he said. "It is all passion just the same. When you are in my arms, what will I care what murderous thoughts are in your breast?"

He reached out a hand as if he would caress her hair. She shrank back from his touch.

"Never," she said, unable to keep the loathing from her voice. "You will never hold me in your arms."

"I have done so before," he said. "If I so chose, I could do so again."

She turned to run from the room.

"Do you think your husband would refuse me even that?" he asked in a whisper.

His words held her there. Would Joseph dare to refuse him anything? Had she the courage to challenge that dare?

Suddenly he had come to her, his hands were upon her. He tried to turn her so that he could kiss her. Sick with disgust she fought against him. Neither of them spoke a word, it was like a pantomime struggle. She felt his lips upon her bare shoulder. She brought her foot up and kicked his shin. He gave a yelp of pain and flung her from him. She staggered and fell to the floor, knocking over a little French table as she fell.

"It is your choice to make," he said, looking angrily down at her. "I will have you or your husband. It is up to you, but I caution you, do not expect me to wait much longer."

With that he strode from the room, leaving her lying in a crumpled heap on the floor.

Chapter 18

She buried her face in her hands and began to cry hopelessly. What could she do against him? To whom could she turn?

She heard a footstep. Thinking he had come back to torment her further she sat up, cowering against the corner of a divan. It was Mrs. Conners who came in.

"Why, ma'am," she said, surprised to find her mistress in such a condition. "Whatever is the matter? What's wrong?"

Her voice was so gentle, her concern so genuine, that the last of Liza's tenuous restraint vanished. Here was someone at least in whom she could confide, to whom she could unburden her troubled heart, someone good and kind who would care, if nothing more.

She was so touched that she began to cry more loudly. For a moment Mrs. Conners hesitated. After all, this was her employer, and she was only a housekeeper. But she was too tenderhearted to watch such unhappiness without being moved by it, without doing what she could to comfort her. She knelt and took the distraught woman into her arms, cradling her as if she were a small child. The patrician head lay on her work-bent shoulder.

"There, there," she crooned, patting Liza's dark hair until at length the sobs began to subside and the body ceased to tremble.

Slowly, with faltering words at first, Liza began to talk of her unhappiness and the cause of it. At first Mrs. Conners was embarrassed at being the recipient of such private confidence from a woman so far above her station. But as she listened, her shock and her fear outweighed her natural reticence.

Later, Mrs. Conners brought her mistress tea, into which she poured a little brandy. She coaxed her to drink some of it. Liza made little protesting noises, but she did as she was bade.

"You've been so kind," Liza murmured, sipping the tea.

"It's nothing," Mrs. Conners said. She was too numb from the story she had been told to be more talkative than that.

Liza sighed and said, "If only there were something we could do."

Mrs. Conners's heart sank lower still at

the use of the plural pronoun. There it was, now it was *her* problem as well, and Lord in Heaven, how could she be expected to handle anything like this?

Her faith was simple and strong. She did not for a moment question the story she had heard. She had seen and heard things since she had been at Sea Cliff, more than she had let on to anyone. And she knew well enough that evil existed, just as surely as good did. She knew that love could be the greatest evil of all, for life had taught her that.

That there was a devil she questioned no more than that there was a God, and in her mind they were ever at war over the souls of mankind. She believed that one was afflicted, but that one had only to endure, to resist and in time God would make it right, if not this side of death, then beyond.

But she had never had to endure anything like this. Precious Savior, what did she know of valuable rubies and great wealth? It was all beyond her limited experience, beyond her ability to comprehend it even. The details of the story blurred in her mind, into a great cloud of evil that threatened this woman before her, and through her, threatened herself and her children as well. And what could she do?

"There is one thing," she said finally.

Liza looked up, hope at once springing to life in her tear-reddened eyes.

"What is that?" she asked. It was a relief at last to have shared her unhappiness, to have someone with whom she could at least discuss the situation. And she trusted instinctively in Mrs. Conners's inherent goodness.

"It's Christmas Eve. I had planned on going to church in a little while."

"May I go with you?" Liza asked shyly.

"I think that you ought, ma'am," Mrs. Conners said somberly.

Chapter 19

It did not seem strange to Liza that she should be going to church on Christmas Eve with her housekeeper. So much had happened that was unreal, so much of her life had turned upside down, that the conventions seemed no longer to matter.

She felt better even before they left for the church. She had unburdened her soul, nor did she give a thought to the burden she had placed on that of her companion. They rode through the snowy streets and for the first time in weeks Liza felt a sense of tranquillity.

It was snowing, great tufts of white that swirled and fluttered briefly in the coach lights. The snow had turned everything clean and pure. Nearly everyone was at home by now and it was still except for the bells of the churches and the *clop-clop* of the horses' hooves. They passed lighted windows in which she could see Christmas trees and families gathered together before the fire. It gave her a pang to see them, secure, safe, happy, while she was isolated by her knowledge of evil.

"But not," she told herself gratefully, "completely isolated." She reached across the seat and patted Mrs. Conners's hand.

The church was crowded with other worshippers. They found a place near the rear. The organ music swelled, and soon from the rear came the stately procession. It was a sensual experience and Liza gave herself up to it — the incense, the gleaming crucifix, the boys with their shimmering candles; the young priests, their faces no more touched with sin than those of the boys; and finally the bishop himself, grandly blessing the crowd as he passed.

Dominus vobiscum . . .

With her conscious mind she took part in the mass, but another part of her turned deeply inward, searching within herself for the answer she needed.

"Blessed Father," she prayed, "If there is another way, show it to me."

But no answer came, and at last she knew that there was but one answer. She had prayed before to God to show her some way to save her husband, and the devil had shown her a way.

What could she do? If Joseph were drowning, if he were in any physical danger, she would gladly risk her own life to save him, give up her life, even. Now he was in a danger that went far beyond physical danger; much more than his life on this earth was at stake. And it was in her power to save him.

And save him, she vowed, she would. At any cost to herself.

She closed her mind to what that cost would be. Perhaps she had known all along that in the struggle between herself and Al Zaghral, he would eventually win. But she was prepared to lose, because she had realized that if she failed to try to save Joseph, the soul she had kept for herself would be of no value anyway.

The mass ended. People were leaving, hurrying now because it was Christmas Eve and they wanted to be home with their families, enjoying the holiday. Liza rose. Beside her Mrs. Conners got to her feet as well. Together they joined the throngs of people moving toward the exit door.

"Wait," Mrs. Conners said at the door. She disappeared back into the interior of the church. Liza stepped aside, pulling her coat tightly about her as the cold wind blew against her. In a moment the housekeeper rejoined her and they went down the wide steps together.

The carriage had waited for them. It was

welcome after their walk through wind and snow. Liza sank back into the seat and closed her eyes. She was resigned to her fate, and even impatient to get on with it. "If it were done when 'tis done, then 'twere well it were done quickly."

Joseph was at home when they arrived. He was in the parlor, drink in hand, staring morosely into the fire. Liza shed her outer garments quickly and came into the room, her cheeks still flushed from the cold.

The sight of him renewed her hope; there was still one alternative left to her. If she could persuade him to give her the ruby, perhaps she could save him without submitting to Al Zaghral's wicked designs. And for the moment he was alone.

He turned as she came in. Something in the way he looked at her touched her deeply.

"Joseph," she murmured and came into his arms.

"Merry Christmas, darling," he said, kissing her, and she replied, with a break in her voice, "Merry Christmas to you, too."

After a long moment she said, still holding her cheek pressed against his strong chest. "I want to ask you something . . . I want you to do something for me."

"If I can, I will," he said.

"There's something I want you to give me, as a Christmas present."

She felt him relax slightly at that remark. He said, "Anything money can buy is yours. You have only to name it."

"This is . . . not something that can be bought," she said. "It is something you already own."

He held her back at arm's length and looked down into her face. "Tell me," he said.

"Give me the ruby," she said. She saw the shock register on his face, and went on quickly, "Darling, you said you would give me anything, and that is what I want. Surely it can't matter to you now, you have so much wealth already."

"Liza, I don't understand, what can you possibly want with the stone?" he asked.

She pulled away from him. "Perhaps there are things that I want," she said, turning her back. "Why should I be only a pale reflection of my husband, when I could have wealth of my own, or power of my own? Perhaps I want fame. I might be a great actress on the stage, or a famous singer in the opera. I don't suppose you've ever thought that I might have dreams of my own."

She was speaking coldly. She knew that

everything might depend upon how well she played this scene, and she put everything that she had into it. She turned back to him and her eyes flashed as if she were genuinely angry with him.

"A woman is a person, too," she said. "There are things that I want, too."

"I've given you everything you ever said you wanted," he said, stung by her remarks.

She thought of the peace of mind she had wanted through the last few months, the security, the safety. "No," she said aloud. "Not everything."

"I'm sorry," he said, refilling his wine glass. "I had no idea how you felt."

She went to him and put her hand on his broad shoulder. "Then you'll give me the ruby," she said, hardly daring to hope.

He shook his head. "I can't do that," he said.

"Then you don't love me at all!" she cried.

"Liza, Liza, I do, believe me I do!" he said in a voice filled with anguish.

"If you loved me, you would give me the stone."

For a moment they faced one another. Mrs. Conners, who had been a silent witness to the scene, understood what Liza was trying to do, and was torn in two by her own feelings. Her instinct was to cheer on a woman so brave; but she knew that victory for her meant untold tragedy.

"Holy Father," she prayed silently. "What are we to do?"

"Liza," Joseph said in a gentle, coaxing voice, "I cannot do what you ask. Even if it was in my power to give you the ruby, and I don't know that it is, I could never condemn you to what I have suffered, to what I know you would have to suffer as well."

"And have you suffered, Joseph?" she asked softly.

"I can tell you this," he said, taking her hand in his, "That no amount of wealth or power is worth the cost of that ruby. It means the loss of your soul. I cannot allow you to agree to that."

"If I may be permitted."

It was Al Zaghral. Even Mrs. Conners, still by the door, had not heard him approach. He was not human; he seemed to arrive like a gust of wind, suddenly, soundlessly. Frightened by him, she moved quickly aside, but he hardly noticed her. His attention was all for the couple in the room.

Joseph put his arm protectively about Liza and drew her closer. Together they faced their enemy.

"I could not help but overhear your conversation," he said, advancing into the room. "You," he said to Joseph, "were right in questioning whether the ruby was yours to give. It is not, of course. It is yours only so long as I allow you to retain it — and you know what the end of that possession will signify."

"Yes," Joseph said. "And I wish it were now. I want to be done with it."

Al Zaghral smiled. "There is no need to be in a hurry," he said. "Everything in its own time."

"And you," he said, addressing Liza with a faint bow, "I have told you before that the ruby is mine, mine alone. It is only loaned to others, and it is I who decides to whom it shall be loaned, and under what terms. Of course, as I told you before, if you truly desire the stone, I will give it to you."

She met his insinuating gaze boldly. "I desire it," she said.

He smiled again, an evil smile, and nodded his head. "And you understand the price?"

"Fully."

"Then," he said, offering her his hand, "come with me, and I promise you that the stone shall be yours before the night is ended."

She shrank from his touch. Far from being offended by her revulsion toward him, he only seemed to be amused.

"No, not yet," she said. "I want some time with my husband first. Come to my room in . . . in one hour. I will be there."

"Oh, Liza," Joseph said with a moan. He shook his head.

"I will be there," she repeated firmly, looking steadily at the other man.

"I will come," Al Zaghral said. He bowed to each of them again and left the room.

"Liza, Liza," Joseph said.

"It's all right," she told him, "I'm not afraid. But please, hold me in your arms. We've only an hour left."

Chapter 20

Hardly any of them had been aware of Mrs. Conners's presence in the room. She had watched the drama unfolding before her eyes; now she stood for a moment longer by the door, regarding the young couple as they embraced one another lovingly. Then, faintly embarrassed at being a witness to their whisperings of love, she left them alone.

She went along the hall and up the wide stairs, frowning as she went in the direction her thoughts were taking.

Of course she knew what she must do, there was really no choice, but Lord in Heaven, how had she ever gotten herself entangled in such a situation?

"This is what comes of getting involved," she told herself, "of becoming obligated to another person."

She should never have let Mrs. Hanson do favors for her in the beginning, it weakened a person's position and eventually it destroyed you. One thing led to another. All of her life she had fought against being obligated to anyone.

Now she was involved, hopelessly committed. She would have to do something to save them and she despised herself for it. What of her own life, after all, and what of her children's lives?

But she already knew the answer to that, she had faced the truth of the situation while she had prayed at church. Her life, and her children's lives, were no longer hers. Mrs. Hanson had already bought them with all of her favors.

As for the children, what life had they had before Mrs. Hanson had come into it? They had had nothing, and now they had a great deal. And for the rest of their lives Mrs. Hanson would care for them now. She would have to. Mrs. Conners would see to that, she would guarantee it — by making Mrs. Hanson in turn forever obligated to them, to her.

"They'll have everything," she told herself, as if it were a charm against evil.

She went to Glade's room first and woke him, and told him to dress and come to Jessie's room. He did not question her, he rarely did. He sat up, awake at once, and nodded solemnly to her instructions. As she left she heard him already clambering out of bed.

Jessie was delighted by this midnight diversion. "What is it?" she asked in an excited whisper, "Are we going to see Santa Claus?"

"I'm afraid not, darling," Mrs. Conners replied. "We've already missed him. See, he's been here already."

She had gone to her own room and fetched the gifts she had gotten for them. Now she spread them on the floor; they were few enough, but so much more than previous years that they seemed bounteous indeed.

"Oh, Momma, are they all for us?" Jessie squealed with delight.

"Yes, dear," Mrs. Conners said. "Glade, aren't you going to open yours?"

Glade had been eyeing the packages suspiciously, as if trying to understand what their significance was. He gave her a puzzled look now.

"It's all right, really," she said, patting his shoulder. "Open your presents, please."

He did as she said, gravely examining each gift as he unwrapped it. For him there was a long knitted muffler and gloves that matched and of course a book; for Jessie a pretty hat with flowers made of ribbons and mittens, and a doll house. She had spent most of the salary the Hansons were paying her on these few presents.

Jessie squealed with delight over her presents and had to run immediately and fetch her doll so that she too could have a look at the new house.

"Excuse me a moment, please," Glade said, standing.

"Why, where are you going?" his mother asked. "I was going to sing a carol."

"I'll be right back," he said. He disappeared back to his own room before she could question him further.

He was back in a moment with a crudely wrapped package. He stood before where she knelt on the floor and handed it wordlessly to her.

With hands that trembled she tore away the wrappings to reveal a wooden box. That Glade had made it himself was evident and that it was made from pieces of scrap wood was evident as well. It was simply fashioned, its only decoration her initials carved in the lid, and it was small, not much bigger than her hand. He had oiled the wood; she could still smell faintly the scent of the oil he had used, and the surface of the wood was sleek to the touch.

"It's a jewel box," Jessie said proudly. "Glade made it himself."

The mother opened the lid. Inside a piece of dress material had been glued to the bottom for a lining. It was wrinkled, and a trail of glue ran down one side.

"I glued the lining in," Jessie said unnecessarily.

"Maybe someday," Glade said, "We can buy you the jewels to put in it."

She could not fight back the tears. "My darlings," she murmured, putting her arms about them and hugging them to her breast, "you are the jewels of my life."

For a long moment they stayed like that, locked in a mutual embrace. She would have liked to remain like that forever, but at last she remembered. Time was running short.

This, she thought, is the picture they would hold of one another ever after, throughout eternity. She released them from her embrace.

"Shall we sing a carol now?" she asked.

"There's no Christmas tree," Jessie objected.

She hesitated for a moment. "The angels had only a light for the first Christmas," she said, going for a candle, "but it was the light of love, and so shall ours be."

She lighted the candle and set it on the floor before them. Its flame flickered unsteadily for a moment, then rose up straight and golden. Its light was a sheen of gold on the children's faces.

They joined their hands together, forming a circle around the candle, and began to sing.

"Silent night, holy night;
All is calm, all is bright . . ."

The master was alone in the parlor when she came down. For a moment she hesitated in the doorway. He was sitting sunk in his chair, his face buried in his hands. He looked utterly pathetic, and utterly defeated.

Some instinct told him finally that she was there. He looked up, hardly seeming at first to recognize her. She knew that he had always resented her, although she did not know why.

"My wife has just stepped out of the room for a moment," he said, as if he wanted to get rid of her. "She'll be right back."

"That's all right," she said, stepping into the room. "It's you I want to see."

Chapter 21

The hall was dark, her room even darker. Al Zaghral pushed the door wide and stood in the doorway. His senses were keen, and now he strained to penetrate the darkness.

At first he thought that she was not there, that her courage had failed her after all. Then there was a faint movement near the window, and he saw her standing there; she was no more than a shadow among shadows. He smiled in triumph, and came toward her.

"You are mine," he said into the darkness.

"Not yet," she whispered, and tension made her voice sound unlike her own. "The ruby?"

"I have brought it," he said, coming to a stop before her.

He held his hand out and slowly uncurled his fingers. The stone lay upon the palm of his hand. Even in this gloom it seemed to glow with its eerie light, a beacon lighting the way to hell and eternal damnation.

"Here it is," he said. He saw a movement as she reached for it. "But know and be certain, once you have taken it in your hand," he said, "you are mine, body and soul, for all eternity."

For a fraction of a second the hand paused in midair. Then her fingers closed about the gem, claiming it.

"God's love is beyond eternity," she said.

The faint touch of her fingers against his hand set a warning bell ringing in his mind. These were not her hands, soft as the wings of a dove, lovely as the first blush of the rose. These hands were hard and cracked, old with more than time alone. And that voice, still a whisper, to disguise it perhaps . . .

He seized a bony wrist in an iron grip and drew her roughly to the window. Seizing a curtain, he tore it aside to let the moonlight into the room.

It was not her at all, but the other one, the housekeeper, Mrs. Conners. He gave a snarl of anger. "You?" he cried. "What are you doing here?"

She held the ruby clenched tightly in her fist. "Damning my soul," she said evenly. "But saving hers — and his."

"Your soul?" he roared, half-flinging her against the wall. "Your soul? I have no need of your soul, witch. You think to trick *me*, Eblis? I will tear you limb from limb, and when I am finished, I will have the stone again, and I'll have that foolish woman. Give me the ruby, now."

"No," she said, drawing back from him.

He raised a hand — she could not imagine what he intended to do, nor did she plan to wait. Her soul might be his, but her life was still her own, and so would her death be.

She lifted her other hand and threw into his face the vial of water she held there, the holy water she had brought from the church.

"Precious Father," she prayed, yanking her hand free from his, "give me one minute, only one." She turned from him and ran from the room, lifting her skirts high to give her freedom.

He gave a shriek of pain and horror as the water splashed over his face. It was like the flame of hell licking at his flesh, it burned, it seemed to sear its way through flesh and bone and sinew into the very core of his being.

"Witch," he screamed, pain and rage mingling into the storm of fury. "You'll pay for this, you'll know the terrors of hell!

Run, run anywhere you like, you will never escape me."

Half-blind he stumbled after her from the room, along the corridor and down the stairs. He was in time to see her fling open the front door and race out.

Joseph and Liza were in the hall at the foot of the steps. She looked bewildered.

He paid them scarcely any attention, for suddenly he had had a precognition of what she planned, that creature who had dared to interfere. In his mind's eye he saw her as she was, racing with all the strength she could muster toward the cliff's edge.

"No!" he cried, and raced after her.

Staring as Al Zaghral raced by, Liza could hardly grasp what was happening. "Joseph," she said, shaking her head as if to clear her thoughts. "What is it, what's happening?"

He looked not at all confused, but wore a weary expression. "She wanted to save you," he said. "And me."

"But . . ." Suddenly she saw, and it gave her a shudder of terror. "Oh, Joseph, we must help her."

Without waiting for his reply, she too began to run out into the night. Joseph did not follow her; he knew too well that they could never stop that evil creature. For a moment or two he had dared to hope that Mrs. Conners's scheme might work, that Eblis would settle for her soul, and they, or at least Liza, would be spared. But Eblis's cry of rage from upstairs had told him that hope was futile.

On and on she ran, not daring to count the yards that still separated her from the cliff's edge. She knew that he was in pursuit, but it seemed to be a dark wind that raced after her, a storm of rage. She could all but feel his hot breath on the back of her neck, and she prayed silently that God would give her legs the strength she needed.

And there at last was the end, near, nearer still. And suddenly she knew, knew within her heart, that he would not reach her in time. But she knew something more as well, something that eased the pain burning in her breast.

Her soul was not his. It never had been. It never could be. That was only a trick, the last and worst cruel trick of the devil to bend you to his will, his assurance that he would own your soul. But it was not man's to give, nor the devil's to take — the soul was what it had always been, the breath of God within.

With that thought in her heart and a smile on her face she threw herself over the edge, into the waiting darkness below.

He reached for her, and missed. He gave a shriek of rage and stood on the edge of the cliff staring down, watching her as she fell.

"Curse you," he cried, shaking his fist. "Curse you forever!"

But his curse fell on deaf ears.

Then he too threw himself over the cliff's edge, to the rocks below, and the pounding ocean.

Liza, running vainly after them, slowed and stopped, gasping for breath. She tried to scream as Mrs. Conners disappeared over the cliff, but no sound came forth. She heard Al Zaghral's cry of rage and his curse, and she saw him too leap to his death.

It was done. They were gone. She walked slowly to the edge and gazed down. Below she could see nothing, only the faint glow of the whitecaps as the surf pounded the rocks.

Eblis was gone, and his cursed stone with him. The nightmare had ended.

And Joseph? That thought was like a fresh breath of air that filled her with new hope and sent her hurrying back toward the house. The door stood open where they had rushed out.

"Joseph," she called his name as she ran up the steps, and again, "Joseph," this time a cry of dismay. He was lying on the floor in the corridor, as if he were dead. For a moment she thought that Eblis had claimed him after all.

"My darling," she sobbed and ran to him. Kneeling beside him she cradled his head in her arms and held him to her.

He stirred slightly in her arms. He was not dead after all, only unconscious. She clung to him and whispered a prayer of thanks.

"Liza," he murmured.

His eyes opened. She looked into them and saw shame and regret and repentance, and she knew that his soul was his own again — battered and bruised, true, even stained, but it would heal. He would be his own man again, his own, and hers.

"Joseph," she said, and kissed him thankfully.

Epilogue

A young man and a young woman were walking along the beach. It was early morning, and there was a delicious sense of wickedness at being out like this, unchaperoned, unobserved. He brought his lips close to her ear and whispered to her, and she blushed and made as if to slap him, but she tittered with pleasure and mirth nonetheless.

Suddenly she stopped and gave a little cry of surprise. "Look," she said, pointing. "What is that?"

He looked too, and gasped. It was a gem, the largest he had ever seen, and the most brilliant. It shone in the morning sunlight like a beacon, leading them directly to itself.

"It's . . . it's beautiful," she said when he had picked it up and held it in his hand. "Is it genuine, do you think?"

"Do you think a piece of glass could shine like this?" he asked, a bit sharply.

"What do you suppose we should do with it?" she asked.

"I don't know." He turned the stone round and round in his fingers; he could hardly take his eyes off it.

"Someone must have lost it," she said, and added, without conviction. "Maybe we ought to try to find the owner."

"It must be worth a fortune," he said; he had scarcely heard her. He scarcely remembered that she was there.

"If I may be permitted," a low voice said from behind them.

They whirled about, startled; they had been so absorbed in their find that they had heard no one approach. A man stood just at their backs, a dark-skinned man in a black suit, but with an eastern turban on his head. He smiled and bowed toward them.

"It is a lovely stone, is it not?" he said.

"What stone do you mean?" the young man asked, holding his hand behind him.

The stranger only laughed softly. "But please," he said. "I do not mean to take it from you."

The young man brought his hand slowly out, and opened his fingers. The ruby gleamed hypnotically in his hand. He turned it about, and an answering light flickered for a moment in his eyes.

The stranger smiled. He knew that

light — it was the gleam of greed, of lust, of envy. He knew it well.

"Who are you?" the young man asked, finally looking at him again.

"Your servant," he said, and bowed low again.